Empty World

Also by John Christopher

The "Tripods" trilogy
THE WHITE MOUNTAINS
THE POOL OF FIRE
THE CITY OF GOLD AND LEAD

The "Prince" trilogy
THE PRINCE IN WAITING
BEYOND THE BURNING LANDS
THE SWORD OF THE SPIRITS

THE GUARDIANS
(Winner of The Guardian Award: 1971)
THE LOTUS CAVES
WILD JACK
DOM AND VA

Empty World

JOHN CHRISTOPHER

E. P. Dutton New York

First published in the U.S.A. 1978 by E. P. Dutton,
a Division of Sequoia-Elsevier Publishing Company,
Inc., New York

Library of Congress Cataloging in Publication Data

Christopher, John.   Empty World.

SUMMARY: When a deadly virus kills off most of the
world's population, a teenaged boy tries to survive
in a seemingly empty England.
[1. Survival—Fiction.   2. Science fiction]   I. Title.
PZ7.C457Em   1978   823'.9'14   [Fic]   77-18917
ISBN: 0-525-29250-0

Printed in the U.S.A.
10 9 8 7 6 5 4 3

Empty World

ONE

They were driving along the motorway on a bright sunny morning, everyone happy. While Neil's father drove, his mother was telling him something about a dance at the golf club. Amanda and Andy were arguing, but amiably, about a pop programme they had watched on TV. Grandpa and Grandma were admiring the countryside, he pointing out a view that attracted him and she agreeing. Neil himself was silent, engrossed in a strange but satisfying feeling of well-being. He tried to work out what had given rise to it, but could not. It being end of term, the try he had scored in the junior House final, the prospect of summer and the cricket season ahead? Or perhaps just this journey.

He could not decide, but it did not matter. He was relaxing in the enjoyment of that, too — it not mattering — when he heard his mother's small gasping cry and looked up to see it: the monstrous hulk of the heavy lorry and trailer jack-knifing across the road in front of them, looming up and up. . . . Then screams, and blackness, and he woke up sweating, his fingers digging into the bed clothes that were wrapped tightly round him.

Neil thought about the dream later that day, as he walked across the churchyard on his way to catch the bus

1

to school. It had been full of inaccuracies and impossibilities, the way dreams were. Not a sunny morning, but a dull rain-bleared afternoon. Not a motorway, but the A21, a few miles south of the Tonbridge bypass. And, of course, Grandpa and Grandma had not been there. The Rover was a roomy car, but not that roomy; and besides, the object of the journey had been to spend the weekend with them at Winchelsea.

But the rest – his mother's soft cry, the sight of the monster twisting incredibly across their path . . . was that the way it had been? He had no way of knowing, no recollection of the time between setting out from the house in Dulwich and waking in a hospital bed with a nurse, young, dark and pretty, bending over and smiling and telling him he was all right, and not to worry. He had wondered what she was talking about, and asked what he was doing there; and she had told him again not to worry about anything but to lie back and rest, and he would have visitors very soon.

Neil walked through the crumbling stone archway into the empty shell of what had been the nave of the church before it was destroyed in the French wars. That was nearly seven hundred years ago. Winchelsea then had been a thriving town, recently rebuilt here on its hill after the sea swallowed up old Winchelsea – like its sister-town, Rye, a brash newcomer to the company of the Cinque Ports and hopeful of outstripping its seniors in trade and prosperity. But the sea which destroyed the first port had capriciously moved away from the second, remaining as no more than a mocking gleam on the horizon.

So the hopes had come to nothing, and the traders had gone with the sea. Only a few squares were left of the grid pattern which had made the town a contemporary showplace of planning; and those were occupied by sleepy houses, fronted by lawns and flowers, three or four small shops, a couple of pubs. There had been no point in rebuilding the nave of the church, and the New Gate, which had marked the southern limits of Winchelsea, and through which one summer morning late in the thirteenth century the French had been treacherously admitted, stood now over a muddy lane, nearly a mile out in the country, surrounded by grazing sheep.

There were not many young people in Winchelsea. It was a place for retirement – that was why his grandparents had come to live in it. And in the past, although he had liked visiting them, Neil had felt a kind of impatience. Nothing happened here or was likely to happen, beyond the slow change of the seasons. He looked at the white facades of the houses making up the sides of the great square of the churchyard. Even the post-war ones had an appearance of having been there forever.

He thought of the dream, and then of Grandpa coming to his bedside in the hospital. He had asked Neil how he was, and nodded when he said he had a headache.

"A touch of concussion, but they tell me you're sound in wind and limb."

His grandfather, a Civil Servant until his retirement, was a tall thin man, with a long face lengthened further by a white pointed beard. Although he liked them both, Neil preferred him to his grandmother because he never fussed and talked directly, paying little regard to differences in age. His manner had always been calm and easy. He was trying to look calm and easy now, but not managing. Neil asked him:

"What happened?"

"What have they told you?"

"Nothing. I've not been awake long."

"There was a smash. You don't remember it?"

His tone was even but Neil was conscious of the strain behind it. He thought of them all setting out together after lunch – Amanda insisting on going back to say another goodbye to Prinny, the cat, and worrying in case Mrs Redmayne might not remember to come in and feed him. . . . He said sharply:

3

"Where's Mummy? Is she in hospital, too?" He realized, for the first time properly, that the other beds in the ward were occupied by strangers. "And Amanda, and Andy?"

"They're all right. Don't worry, Neil."

There had been a hesitation, though; very slight, but enough to make the reassurance meaningless. And what he said was meaningless, anyway; because if they had been all right his mother would have been here, beside his bed. He said, hearing his voice echo as though far off:

"All of them?" He stared up at his grandfather. "Dad, as well?"

"They're all right," his grandfather repeated.

He did not need the sight of the tear rolling down the wrinkled cheek to give the lie. Nor did he resent it, knowing the lie was meant to help him, to ease him back into a world that had shattered and changed. But he could not go on looking at another human being. He turned and buried his head in the pillow, immobile, believing and not believing, while his grandfather's voice went on and on and he heard it without listening, an empty noise.

There were others from the Comprehensive waiting at the bus stop. He knew them slightly, and nodded to one or two, but did not engage in conversation. There had been the curiosity one could expect over a newcomer but he had done little to satisfy it; and when the suspicion which was also inevitable had hardened into something more like hostility, he had not minded.

It was a big change from London, and Dulwich College. There had been a talk with his grandfather about that. It seemed the Head had offered to find him one of the few boarding places, and his grandfather had put the proposition to him: he could choose between taking it, and keeping a continuity in school at least, or going as a day boy to the Comprehensive School in Rye.

"Your home's with us now, Neil," Grandpa had said,

4

"and we're very glad to have you – glad for our own sakes. But we're old, and a bit dull, and so is Winchelsea. You might find it better to carry on at Dulwich where there are people you know – chaps your own age."

"No, I'll stay here."

"If you're thinking of the fees, that's not important. You know. . . ."

"No."

He said it brusquely. He had heard his grandparents talking one evening, quietly when they thought he was asleep. There would be a lot of money coming his way. His father, an insurance executive, had himself been more than amply insured. The sole survivor of the family was going to be rich.

The new school was very different from the old, but a large part of the difference, he realized, lay in himself. At Dulwich he had made plenty of friends – more than Andy who, though a year older, was more reserved. And Andy had not been much interested in sports, while he played most games reasonably well.

He had taken part in a couple of cricket games at Rye, and not done badly. But he had kept to himself and the other players, after one or two small overtures, had let him get on with it. It had been the same in school generally. Although it was never mentioned, he guessed the story of what had happened, the reason for his coming here, had got around. He had had one or two pitying glances from girls, and once found a conversation abruptly switched off as he entered a class-room. But no questions were asked, and he volunteered no information.

So he had made no friends, but did not mind it; nor did he miss the ones he had left behind. It was not that he brooded over the disaster. It surprised him to what extent he was able to put it out of his mind; and in spite of occasional lurching moments of fear and sickness, he did not feel particularly unhappy.

He had an idea it would not have been so easy in

London. The impatience he had once felt for the slowness and dullness of the little town had been replaced by a kind of contentment. It was good that nothing happened, and that the most usual sight was of an old man or woman creeping along on some unhurried errand. He liked the quiet empty evenings, with the darkness lit only by chinks of light from cosy sitting rooms, and the single street lamp on the corner.

The others who were at the bus stop had collected into a group and were talking and laughing. He did not know what the subject of conversation was, and did not care. He thought of his dream again, and felt sweat cold down his back, but both dream and reality seemed far away. As the bus came growling down the road from Hastings, through an avenue of leafy green, he found himself whistling. He realized it was the tune Amanda had been so crazy about the last few weeks, but went on.

In general the work seemed easier in Neil's new school, but perhaps because of that less interesting. An exception was Biology, taught by a small stocky man with a Scottish accent and a tendency to range widely round his subject. Today they were dealing with cell structures, and Mr Dunhill moved on to a discussion of the ageing process. There was some evidence, he pointed out, for believing that ageing was caused by the increasing inability of cells to remember the functions laid down for them in the genetic blueprint, a sort of cellular amnesia.

Someone asked if that meant that if something could be done to improve the memory of cells the ageing process could be halted – even reversed? Did it mean people might be able to live forever, barring accidents?

"Well, no, I wouldn't hazard that."

Mr Dunhill rubbed his palms together in front of his chest, a characteristic gesture. He went on:

"But there's an interesting example in the opposite direction, in that epidemic they had in India, a few months back."

The Calcutta Plague, it had been called, because that was where the first cases had occurred. It had swept through northern India, killing hundreds of thousands, and then died out. Neil remembered his father and mother discussing it one evening when he came downstairs after finishing his prep. Their preoccupation, he recalled, had given him the chance of slipping out to a friend's house, without their realizing how late it was.

"You'll remember there were two phases of the disease," Mr Dunhill said. "Initially there was a fever, followed by recovery and a symptomless period varying between ten days and three weeks. That was followed by a general deterioration of bodily functions, leading to collapse and death.

"The striking thing was that the second phase strongly resembled an accelerated ageing process. It mimicked a rare disorder called progeria, specifically the Hutchinson-Gilford syndrome, in which children grow old before they grow up. There was a well-known case of a child in Brazil, who at six months had adult teeth already yellowing, at two years white hair, thinning on top, and who died at ten of hardening of the arteries.

"Fortunately in this case it was not the young who were affected but the old, chiefly the very old. Mostly the victims were over sixty. There were one or two cases as young as the middle forties, and the results there were much more striking: wrinkling of skin, whitening of hair roots, calcium loss, atherosclerosis. It was as though they were racing towards the grave, instead of indulging in that slow crawl which satisfies us normal geriatrics."

Mr Dunhill was in his fifties. It was probably as much as forty years since he had sat in a class-room, listening to someone as old as he was now. Was the joke about being a geriatric as light-hearted, Neil wondered, as it seemed? People died: he had come to know that in the last few weeks in a way he had never known before. And they must fear it, he supposed, more and more as the inevitability drew closer.

"It's a tenable explanation," Mr Dunhill went on, "that the Calcutta virus attacked the individual cells in such a way as to inhibit or destroy that memory function we have been talking about. The victims quite literally died of nothing except old age."

"They were old already, though."

That was someone called Barker, a gangling boy with an almost perpetual silly grin. Mr Dunhill looked at him with distaste.

"Yes, they were, weren't they? And they were only Indians, after all. Nothing to cause us concern. Now let's get back to the mechanism of mitosis."

There was a girl in the class called Ellen, pretty in a fair, frail way. Neil had noticed her chiefly in the company of Bob Hendrix, who was more conspicuous. He was heavily built and had a loud aggressive voice. His hair was bright red, and he usually wore a canary-yellow waistcoat. His father was a prominent Rye tradesman, and he clearly thought deference was due to him on that account.

Hendrix went home for lunch but Ellen, like Neil, stayed at school. On this day she sat near him, and made what appeared to be friendly if timid overtures. He answered her civilly, but without enthusiasm. She persisted, though, and afterwards found him and spoke to him more directly.

"Is it true?" He looked at her. "About your family all being killed?"

It was something he had reckoned on happening but had hoped, with the lapse of time, might not. It was not that he dreaded the reference – more a feeling of embarrassment in advance. Now it had happened, though, he found it did not bother him. She seemed sympathetic rather than curious – a nice girl, probably.

8

At any rate, although he did not volunteer much information, he did not snub her. She went on, in a small soft voice, saying what a terrible thing it was, and he found he did not mind that, either.

It was something, she said, which had always been a nightmare with her. She had imagined it hundreds of times, and it had pursued her in dreams. She mostly thought of it as happening at school – of someone coming in to the class and telling her to report to the Headmaster, of going into his study and seeing his face, much graver than usual. And then being told . . . it was always both of them killed together, usually in a car smash.

Once launched she needed no encouragement to go on. She told him about her life at home, and he was a little surprised. She was an only child. Her father, a plasterer, was very strict – he did not allow her out later than ten in the evening, half past nine in winter. Her mother, it seemed, was ill a great deal. She had to get her own breakfast in the morning, and do housework before she came to school.

It did not strike Neil as the sort of home life one would be particularly terrified to lose; nor her parents as justifying such anxious devotion. Her life in fact seemed fairly wretched compared with the one he had known in Dulwich. Yet he had never had the sort of fears she described. Did that mean he had failed to appreciate what he'd got? He felt a vague guilt, and had a panicky moment of wondering if that was why it had happened – if the God in whom he mostly didn't believe had read his ungrateful mind, and casually sent down destruction.

But he had no time to brood on it because at that point Hendrix joined them. He ignored Neil, and said to Ellen:

"I thought I told you I'd see you outside the library at half past?"

His tone was truculent. Ellen did not reply, but looked at Neil. He had an impulse to tell Hendrix to push off, but it was easily controlled.

Hendrix said: "And haven't I told you about hanging

about with other fellers?"

He was not just truculent, but bullying and contemptuous. Ellen looked at Neil again, in direct appeal this time.

Neil had no fear of the other. He was bigger, possibly stronger, but Neil was fairly sure he was no boxer while he had done quite a bit. If this had happened a couple of months ago he knew what he would have done – told Hendrix to shut up, or he'd sort him out.

He supposed really that was what he ought to do now, but he could not be bothered. Neither the girl nor Hendrix meant enough to be worth his getting involved. The girl, after all, had chosen Hendrix in the past, or let herself be chosen by him. It was not his concern, but if he fought Hendrix and beat him it might become so. Her eyes stayed on his face, but he said nothing.

Hendrix said, openly contemptuous of Neil as well:

"Come on. Leave this London wet. It's Geography first and I didn't have time to do any prep last night. We'll go and get yours."

Neil watched them go off together. He was a bit surprised he could feel so detached about it.

He walked back through the churchyard in the late afternoon. The air was windless, warm for early summer, and the crab apple trees were loaded with blossom. Although many of the graves were old, the inscriptions on the stones rendered illegible by time and weather, some were new, and he passed two graves freshly mounded with flowers. The churchyard represented one of the few ongoing enterprises the town still possessed, the only one really.

Neil thought of Ellen and her nightmares, and wondered about them. Perhaps they did not stem, as he had assumed, from love of her parents, but the reverse. Perhaps that was why the daydream was so persistent.

He wondered too what the future would bring, for her

10

and Hendrix. Most likely nothing: they were very young and there was no reason to suppose anything permanent, like marriage, would come of it. Though it might, of course. Hendrix enjoyed bullying, and Neil had an idea that a part of Ellen, at least, liked being bullied. Maybe they *would* marry, and she could change her nightmares to imagining her husband being killed.

Again his thoughts surprised him. He looked up at the sky, nearly cloudless, where – he was fairly sure again – no invisible vindictive God lurked, reading minds and fashioning thunderbolts to toss down. The church was grey and squat, brooding over its generations of worshippers. All around were the quiet houses with, at this moment, not a person in sight. A car revved up the High Street and roared on towards Hastings, leaving velvety silence behind.

Rye was a quiet town after London, but a Babylon compared with Winchelsea. He thought again how glad he was to be here, but thought that even here there were too many people. It would be nice to live on a desert island, with only a parrot for company. Though the parrot wasn't really necessary, either: the sound of the surf or the wind in the palms would be company enough.

His grandmother came out of the kitchen as he let himself in at the front door. She fussed him as usual, and he accepted it as usual, but refused her offer to make him a snack. She was a great believer in nourishment, and seemed to regard the day in school at Rye as roughly equivalent to an ascent of Everest. In the end he escaped on the double plea of not being hungry and having heavy Physics prep to do. She believed in prep as well, though she thought he worked too hard.

That wasn't true, in fact; he was still coasting for the most part, after Dulwich. He worked away steadily, though, glad to have something to occupy his mind so completely but undemandingly. Apart from Physics, there was English and History . . . witches putting the

11

frighteners on Macbeth, Judge Jeffreys decorating the west country with gibbeted rebels. Violent death was something you might as well get used to; it had been around a long time. And only a fool looked for explanations or justifications.

When he had finished he sat for a time, looking out. His room was at the top of the house and quite big. It ran from the front of the house to the back; his bed was under one window, and the desk at which he sat under the opposite one. This looked over the street, if anything so green and flowery could be called a street. Someone drove a car up, and parked it. Mrs Mellor from over the road passed slowly along his field of vision, and disappeared. A tabby cat succeeded her, and all was quiescence again.

Below and faintly he heard the theme music of BBC television news. He might as well go down and watch as not.

In the sitting room his grandfather and grandmother were in their accustomed armchairs, with the third between them left empty for him. Neil stopped in the doorway, to see if there was anything interesting on. It was only something about the Calcutta Plague starting up again, this time in Karachi.

TWO

IT WAS STILL CALLED the Calcutta Plague after it had
spread south to Sri Lanka and leapt across the Indian
Ocean to a new foothold in Mombasa. Sources of infection
were next confirmed in Cairo and Athens. By that time, in
recognition of the fact that airlines provided the main
channels for its advance, strict checks were being applied
to intending travellers.

But however stringent the controls or co-operative the
passengers, it would probably have made little difference.
There was a period of some days, it appeared, prior to the
fever which was the first symptom of illness, during which
the disease was present in latent form; and in that time the
victim was infective. A person conscientiously observing
all the regulations could still have unwittingly had a contact, and be a carrier. And not many were scrupulous.
Apprehension turned to fear and fear to panic as the hold
of the virus spread and tightened.

The Calcutta part of the name was dropped and forgotten. It was simply the Plague now, and people fled blindly
from it, or tried to. The fact that it was the old who were
attacked only made matters worse. The old who were poor

13

were helpless, of course; but by and large the old were richer than the young, and were ready to use their money to escape the invisible death. The risk of carrying the disease to places still free of infection did not weigh too heavily with them.

When its presence was admitted in Frankfurt, the Prime Minister made a speech on television. His manner had the right combination of concern and reassurance. The situation was tragic, but the medical resources of the world were concentrated on seeking a cure. Could anyone believe that science, which had overcome so many of man's afflictions, would fail in this? No effort or expense would be spared; and Britain, with such names as Jenner and Lister and Fleming as proud a part of her tradition as Nelson or Churchill, would make her full contribution to the common task.

Meanwhile we must thank God this little island had been spared the scourge. But thankfulness needed to be matched by vigilance. He paused, impressively, his expression becoming sterner, demonstrating practicality rather than hopefulness. A State of Emergency had been declared, and was effective forthwith. Certain orders were being promulgated by the Home Secretary, and one of these related to admissions to the United Kingdom from abroad. Until further notice no-one aged forty or over would be allowed entry, by any means of transport or from any part of the world.

Neil's grandfather had been diffident about suggesting it, talking round the subject before coming to the point. Which was that the house in Dulwich was being sold. There would be things there Neil might want. If he didn't feel like going back, perhaps he could make a list of what they were?

For his part Neil did not hesitate: he said he would like to go with his grandfather and check things over on the spot. As a result they drove up together in the old Wolseley

14

the following Saturday morning, through showers and bursts of sunshine. Neil noticed that they branched off the A 21 south of Tonbridge and took the A 20 into London; but he did not comment on it.

Although he had spoken firmly, Neil had wondered what it would be like to see the house again. He had a moment's forgetfulness when they turned into a familiar road, only about half a mile from their destination – a confusion with another time he had been taken home by his grandfather – and he imagined them all as being there. It only lasted a fraction of a second. There was the familiar jolt of sickness but that did not last, either. The equally familiar blankness took its place.

They parked in the drive in front of the locked garage, and Grandpa let them in at the front door. The house had a strange musty smell, and although the furniture was still in place their voices seemed to echo. Someone had obviously been in to clean: it was all tidier than Neil remembered. There was a gap in the sitting room where the colour TV had been: it had been rented, and would have gone back to the shop.

While Neil was picking out what he wanted, his grandfather went round the house making a separate list of things to be kept back from the sale of contents. He tackled the ground floor first, and Neil went upstairs. On the first landing the door of his parents' bedroom was open; he looked, then went in.

The beds looked very flat and tidy, and the rugs were neatly in place. His father's slippers were tucked away, side by side, under a corner of the dressing table, and his electric shaver was in its box. On the dressing table his mother's jewel box was locked, but the little silver ring-tree stood beside it. There was one ring on it, the opal which she did not wear because she thought it was unlucky. She always left that out, and he wondered if it had been because she thought the bad luck might spread, by contagion, to the rest.

Neil picked up the ring and held it to the light. Sunshine made the colours dazzle in the stone; he could remember marvelling at that when he was very little, barely able to reach the dressing table top. Bad luck? He looked at the ring a moment longer, then slipped it into his pocket.

In the room he had shared with Andy, Neil set about the main task, picking things out and carrying them downstairs, a few at a time, to make a pile in the hall. Books were the chief problem – deciding which to discard. In the end he was ruthless, keeping only a few he specially liked and a couple with childhood associations – *The Wind in the Willows* and *The Borrowers*.

Andy's things were mixed up with his own. He saw the portable radio Andy had been given for his last birthday, and remembered feeling jealous on that account. He switched it on, and listened to pop music. The number ended, and was followed by a newscast. Something political. A report on special police precautions being taken because of possible violence at a football match.

"Finally, the Plague. Outbreaks have been reported this morning in the Rhineland, and in Zürich and Paris. From Berlin there are unconfirmed reports that the latest victims include people of a younger age group than previously found – a man in his early forties and a woman in her thirties. A medical spokesman from Guy's Hospital suggests that this may indicate the emergence of a more virulent strain of the virus.

"Back now to the Chicken Farmers, and their new single. . . ."

Neil switched off. He stared down at the radio for a moment; then picked it up and carried it to put with the pile in the hall.

His grandfather said: "All done? I'll give you a hand in loading."

They took things out to the car and stacked them in the boot. Neil returned from one trip to find his grandfather

16

holding the radio and looking at it. He knew it had been Andy's; they had gone to Winchelsea just after the birthday, and there had been a minor fuss about it being played all the time. Their eyes met, but nothing was said.

They came out for the last time, and Grandpa pulled the door to behind them. Mr Preston from next door was standing behind the fence. He greeted them, a bit too loudly.

"How are you, Neil? You're looking well, I must say. It's pretty clear the Sussex air agrees with you."

He had always been nervous – Neil remembered his father being gently mocking about it – and was plainly embarrassed by the occasion. He went on, talking rapidly, to ask what the new school was like, had Neil been to Battle to see where Harold was killed by the Norman arrow, was he making lots of new friends . . .?

He looked even more embarrassed after he'd said that: it was too close to the subject that must not be mentioned. Grandpa was looking uneasy, too. He asked Mr Preston about his garden, and the switch in conversation was gladly accepted. Greenfly was a safer topic. They were a plague this year – he had to spray his roses twice a day.

From greenfly they got on to the Plague. Grandpa said that the immigration ban was the first sensible thing the government had done. Mr Preston shook his head.

"Too late."

"That's being unnecessarily pessimistic. This is an island, thank God. There's no reason why controls shouldn't work, if they're properly handled. And people are scared enough now to do a proper job. It's not like rabies. They're dying in Europe by the thousand."

"It's already here."

"Of course it isn't! If it were. . . ."

"There's been nothing in the news, you mean? There won't be, either. The Emergency regulations include press and broadcasting censorship, remember. They've had panic on the other side of the Channel, and they want

17

to avoid it here."

"You always get rumours." Grandpa's tone was cool. "I don't think it helps to listen to them, or spread them."

"It's not rumour." Mr Preston shook his head again. "I know someone who knows – how many cases, which hospitals. . . . We've got it, I tell you."

Grandpa brought the conversation to an end soon after. It wound up on the nervous boisterous note on which it had begun. Mr Preston repeated how glad he was to see Neil looking so well, and hoped he would come and visit them some time. Susan would be sorry she had missed him; she and her mother were out for the day, shopping.

Neil made a polite response. Susan was a year older then he, a bossy girl with a long nose. None of them had been able to stand her and Andy, following a visit to the Zoo, had nicknamed her the Tapir.

On the drive back Grandpa was quiet at first, but later spoke about Mr Preston. Rumour-mongers always flourished at times like this. Some people had a compulsion to invent things.

"I remember in 1940," he said, "when we were expecting the Germans to invade. One night in September I was on Home Guard duty and we heard planes overhead – wave after wave of them, like nothing we'd heard before. Going back home in the early morning I met a woman who told me, quite definitely, that there had been a German landing in Kent, and that a full-scale battle was going on. Deal had been taken, she said. She was an ordinary-looking woman, respectably dressed, not at all hysterical in her manner, and I believed her. It was some hours before I could be sure there wasn't a word of truth in it. There'd been no landing. The planes we'd heard had been bombers, on their way to the first night raid on London."

He drove on a while, before adding:

"In those days spreading rumours was a criminal offence, and I think it ought to be again. But at least we can

18

disregard them. I wouldn't mention this at home, Neil."

He would be thinking of Grandma. Neil said:

"I won't."

"There's absolutely nothing in it. I'm quite certain of that."

Neil realized something else. It was not just consideration for Grandma; he was afraid himself.

He said, fibbing: "Mr Preston always did stretch things. He's well known for it."

"Yes." Grandpa sounded more cheerful. "We've left it a bit late for getting back. I'll tell you what – we'll stop off and have a pub lunch. Good idea?"

The rumours were in Rye when Neil went to school on Monday, and by the time he returned they were in Winchelsea. That night on the News there was a formal government denial. Next day the rumours were even more positive and circumstantial. People were dropping dead in the streets of London . . . an Old Folks' Home in Croydon had been wiped out to the last resident.

In the evening the doctor called to see Neil's grandmother. His grandfather mentioned hesitantly, when Neil got in from school, that she had been feeling unwell and he'd made her go to bed. Neil asked if he should go up and see her but was told she was probably sleeping – she'd had a disturbed night. He went to his own room and got on with his prep. He had nearly finished by the time he heard a car come up the quiet street and stop at the door. He looked out and saw the doctor, a jaunty figure swinging his bag, being admitted.

He was in the sitting room when the doctor came downstairs. Grandpa was there, too, making a poor show of pretending to watch television. He switched off the set and asked, in too casual a voice:

"How is she, then, Alan?"

"Bit of a temperature." The doctor was clipped and cheerful. "Sore throat, aches and pains. Could be 'flu –

19

more likely a head cold."

"Nothing to worry about?" Grandpa went to the sideboard. "Scotch? Water with it?"

"A touch. Whoah. Ah, that's better. I was just about ready for that."

"Busy day?"

"More than somewhat. Fair number of my senior patients down with Plague, or imagining they are. Not difficult to reassure them, but it takes time."

Grandpa said, shamefaced: "Hard on you. But with all the talk. . . ."

"Oh, very understandable. I'm not complaining. Better imaginary illnesses than real."

"If it did come. . . ."

"What? The Plague, you mean?"

"Yes. How would you cope?"

"Oddly enough, fairly easily, I fancy. The initial fever's mild, and there's little you can do about it. Just the usual advice – keep warm, bed rest, plenty of fluids. And there would be even less point in trying to treat the second stage. They die of heart failure usually, not of anything specific. Once it really got going, I doubt if anyone would bother calling us in."

"It may never happen."

"That's a point."

"All this ridiculous talk about it having got to England. . . ."

"But it has." He drained his glass. "More than a score of cases confirmed, and God knows how many in the pipeline. The horse was well and truly home before they locked the stable door."

Grandpa said, in a low voice:

"So what will happen?"

"Chaos, if the experience elsewhere is anything to go by. But it may not reach our little backwater."

"Do you really think not?"

"Viral epidemics build up in densely populated

localities. Like the common cold − carrying all before it in the initial stages and devastating the areas of occupation. Then resistance builds up, the enemy wavers, retreats, vanishes. That's the normal pattern of events."

"You think it may stay confined to the cities?"

"Well, no, but they'll probably bear the brunt. And the more remote the area, the more chance of escaping. Incidentally, talking of people who may be under pressure, I can think of one profession that will know all about it."

Grandpa took the doctor's glass and refilled it.

"Which one is that?"

"Thanks. The undertakers. Medical treatment won't be a problem, but disposal of bodies will. I hear in Germany the crematoria are working flat out, round the clock, and they're still having to dig mass graves. Lime pits, actually."

"Terrible." Grandpa shook his head. "And there's nothing anyone can do?"

"They'll probably come up with a vaccine eventually but the thing's entirely new − nothing to go on. And by the time they do it will most likely have petered out. Leaving a million or so dead."

"Terrible," Grandpa repeated.

"Well, yes. But probably no more so than dying of cold because you can't afford to switch an electric fire on in the winter. Or being beaten to death by thugs for the fifty pence in your purse."

He downed the second drink, and reached for his bag.

"Well, I'd better be hitting the reassurance trail again." He nodded amiably to Neil. "At any rate, you're in a safe age-group."

Neil said: "There have been some cases of younger people getting it, haven't there?"

"Freaks," the doctor said. "And well out of your range, even so. The youngest was thirty seven. That's ancient, wouldn't you say?"

The dam burst two days later with an official admission of the presence of the Plague in Britain. It had also crossed the Atlantic, and was in both North and South America; and despite continuing denials it was believed to have been active for some time behind the Iron Curtain.

The official line now resembled the one the doctor had suggested. The worse the epidemic got, the sooner it would run its course. Meanwhile all possible measures were being taken to control the situation; and the co-operation of the public was sought in helping to get the country through the dark and difficult days ahead. In particular it was urged that older people should only leave their homes when the journey was absolutely necessary. This would give them the best protection personally, and also minimize the risk of spreading the epidemic.

It was not easy to gauge exactly what was going on after that. Official news was scanty, and not only about the position in England: what was happening elsewhere in the world was played down, too. The rumours multiplied, of course. There were stories of lime pits being dug in the London parks, of people fleeing from the unbearable stench of decay in districts where the disposal of bodies had completely broken down. It was said that the Prime Minister was dead, and most of the Cabinet. Certainly he did not appear on television again.

Then suddenly the plague was in Rye, and two days later in Winchelsea. That was the day Mr Dunhill stayed away from school. He was back two days later, and looked no different.

But through the days that followed the class watched him. It was impossible not to, Neil found – impossible not to speculate that he was marked for death, and wonder how soon the end would come. The faces looked at Mr Dunhill and Mr Dunhill looked back at the faces, and talked about Biology. One morning he set an examination, and was scathing about the results. They would need to do a lot better, he said, in the end-of-term examination.

But would he be there to set it – did he himself believe he would?

On Monday morning his appearance was shocking. He looked ten years older at least, and they saw his hands tremble when he went to write on the blackboard. The writing was scrawled and wavering.

During class the Headmaster came in and spoke to him. Their voices were low, but it was obvious that the Headmaster was urging something, Mr Dunhill refusing. It was easy to guess what: that he should do as another master had already done – go home and die in peace, free from watching eyes. But in the end the Headmaster retired, defeated, and Mr Dunhill turned back to face the class.

"Radcliffe, I trust you have used that unexpected break to some advantage." His voice was thinner, but steady. "Perhaps you would be good enough to try again, on that question concerning the structure of the rabbit's eye."

It lasted another two days, during which he continually deteriorated. His skin wrinkled, his voice became more reed-like, his movements tottery and uncertain. In the final lesson the effort to write on the blackboard was too much for him. It was then, sinking into his chair, that he spoke about himself.

"You will, I am sure, have been noting the changes in my appearance – more closely and more accurately, most likely, than I have done by studying my reflection in the looking glass. I wonder if you have pondered an interesting anomaly – that while my skin is wrinkled my hair has not noticeably changed in colour. The emphasis, of course, is on 'noticeably'. The hair roots are quite white. The reason the hair proper, while thinner, is still no more than tinged with grey, is simply that human hair grows at a slower rate than that of the cellular deterioration caused by the Calcutta virus."

He paused, as though speech were becoming wearisome. He made his old gesture of rubbing his palms together, but feebly. He went on:

"It seems that you may shortly be living in a world in which the old have ceased to exist. The middle-aged, too, perhaps, because the number of cases in the thirty plus group seems to be increasing."

He paused again. "This may appear, minor personal considerations on one side, to offer the prospect of a glorious freedom from the tyranny of the older generations. Perhaps it will. On the other hand, it may prove less glorious than you imagine. At any rate, I hope you put your freedom to good use."

Mr Dunhill stood up. "And now, being rather tired, I propose bringing this lesson to a premature end. I shall not be with you tomorrow, but I imagine the loss of tuition in Biology may be one of the smallest of the problems ahead of you. I bid you all goodbye."

Someone mumbled something in reply. The rest of the class watched in silence as he shuffled to the door and, without a backward look, closed it behind him.

THREE

SCHOOL CLOSED at the end of that week; temporarily, it was said, but there was no suggestion as to when it might be re-opened. Things in general were becoming chaotic. There were unexpected power cuts, some lasting for hours, shortages of certain foods and other goods, a growing emptiness of the streets as fewer people ventured out on any but essential business. The green expanse of the Salts, below the town, gradually turned brown as the bulldozers – one of the few remaining indications of activity – scored trenches for the mass graves.

The bus failed to appear on the final day of school, and Neil had to walk the two and a half miles across the Marsh to Winchelsea. As he climbed the steep hill to the town gate a car was travelling erratically down. At one point it was heading straight for him. He found it fairly easy to get out of the way – then watched it crash into the fence, ten yards below, and hang there, suspended over the drop.

He went back to look more closely. It had one occupant, the driver, a desiccated ancient he barely recognized as Mr Behrens, a middle-aged friend of his grandparents. There were no signs of injury, but he was dead.

Since there was nothing he could do, Neil resumed his climb. Winchelsea always had an empty look compared with most places, but the emptiness this afternoon was almost tangible. The day was warm and grey, and one or two large spots of rain splashed as he went along the High Street. The few shops were closed. There was no sound except a lazy twitter of birds. As he passed an open window he caught from within the sickly sweet smell of corruption. A week ago he would not have known it; now he recognized it instantly.

He let himself into the house and called to announce his arrival. His grandfather came into the hall from the sitting room. He had had the fever a week before, and was plainly dying. Neil had thought of asking if there were anything he should do about Mr Behrens, but could not. The body would be found soon enough, and put in the truck that went daily to Rye with the small town's quota of corpses.

Grandpa went through to the kitchen, and Neil followed.

"Your grandmother's not too well." He gestured helplessly at a pile of new potatoes, partly scrubbed. "I was going to make supper for you, but . . ."

"That's all right," Neil said. "Don't worry. I don't feel hungry."

"You must eat." His voice was feebly emphatic. "Keep your strength up."

"I'll do something. Can I get something for you, Grandpa? Or Grandma?"

"No, but. . . . Look after her, will you? It won't be long. I didn't call Dr Ruston: no point. We know what it is this time."

He put a hand unsteadily to the corner of the kitchen table, and sat on one of the stools. Looking up at Neil, he said:

"No complaint, really, for either of us. We've had a long time, and it will be close together. Your grandmother would be lost on her own. But I worry about you."

26

There seemed no point in denials. Neil said:

"Don't worry. I'm all right."

"You're more alone than most . . . after what's happened. But at least things are in order. Penstable in Rye has the details – wills and all that."

Penstable was his grandfather's solicitor. Neil did not speak. His grandfather said:

"I suppose Penstable will go, too, if he hasn't already. But one of the juniors will sort it out. It's fairly simple – everything goes to you."

He paused. "You'll be quite well off. It's controlled till you're twenty, but I've left instructions to them not to be unreasonable." He paused again, breathing heavily. "The main thing is that you'll have enough for a good education – university's an expensive business nowadays. I hope you'll go into a decent profession. You'll want something more than money."

Neil had been listening with numb acquiescence, but said now:

"Stop it!"

He was angry with something or someone, but did not know what or whom. His grandfather said:

"I'm sorry, Neil. It's hard for you."

He took the old man gently by the arm; anger had given way to numbness again. He said:

"Come through to the sitting room, and I'll make us a pot of tea. Tinned milk, I'm afraid."

His grandfather let himself be led and settled into his armchair. The television set came on, signalling the end of another power cut; but the screen stayed blank until Neil switched it off. He wondered if that was temporary, too, or if television had closed down for the duration of the crisis. Not that it mattered.

The following morning his grandfather was dead. Neil knew what would happen if he contacted the emergency burial service: the truck would come round and a couple of

27

men would haul out the sheeted body and put it with the others for consignment to Rye. He could not bear the thought.

He told his grandmother what he proposed, and she turned from looking at the dead face to nod her head. There was a herbaceous border where the digging was fairly easy, and it was close to the back door. There had been rain in the night and the morning was raw and damp, but he found himself sweating as he dug. His grandmother came out of the house and stood close by. She said:

"I'd help, if I could."

Neil paused, wiping sweat from his brow with the back of his hand.

"Go inside, and rest."

She looked down at the trench.

"You'll make it deep enough?"

Deep enough for two, she meant. He said again, but more gently:

"Go inside, Grandma. I'll call you."

When it was done she insisted on helping him to carry out the body and lay it in the grave. She picked up a clod of earth, crumbled it, and threw it on the sheet. She said: "Goodbye, Ted," then turned away and went back into the house. Neil stayed and covered the body with earth.

Neil buried his grandmother a week later. During that time he did not go out except to get food for them both. There were difficulties about that: one of the shops had re-opened, but had scarcely anything on its shelves. He walked out across the fields and found a farmhouse. It seemed to have been deserted: there was no sign of human life and no-one came when he knocked. After he had done that several times without answer, he tried the door. It was only on the latch, and he pushed it open.

A smell of death contended with older smells of polish and leather and cooking, but he saw no bodies downstairs and did not venture higher. In the kitchen there was spoiled food, but beyond there was a larder which yielded cheese and potatoes and a large bowl of eggs which, when he tried them in water, showed their relative freshness by sinking.

He made up a bundle of what he wanted and left three pound notes on the kitchen table, weighted down by a potato. He doubted if there would be anyone to collect them, but it seemed the proper thing to do. He had, anyway, more money than he knew what to do with: his grandfather had drawn several hundred pounds out of the bank a few days before his death.

Going out, he was confronted in the yard by a cow. It mooed hoarsely and sounded distressed, he thought. Its udders were heavily swollen. Neil studied the beast for a moment, then went back into the kitchen. The bucket he had noticed standing upside down on a table looked clean, but he washed it out anyway.

The cow was still there. It lowered its head as he advanced on it, which he found a bit unnerving, but did not move. He spoke to it reassuringly in a low voice, calling it Daisy, and positioned the bucket underneath. The cow mooed again when he put his hands to her udders, and shifted her feet. He thought she was about to make off and had mixed feelings: there was a good supply of tinned milk at home. But she stayed where she was, and his awkward pulling motions, copied from someone he had seen on a TV feature, produced thin uneven squirts of milk which splashed noisily into the bucket, or sometimes missed it and hit the ground.

The operation would have been a lot easier with a milking stool, but it didn't seem worth while going to look for one. They probably didn't exist, now that cows were milked by machine. He had to kneel, with his face against the animal's warm heaving side, shifting position when he got cramped.

With the bucket three quarters full, he had had enough.

The udders still looked gorged, but presumably she felt a little happier. He wondered how many other cows were wandering around in distress; probably thousands, throughout the county. He gave Daisy a farewell slap on the rump and picked up the bucket as she moved away. Milk, he remembered, was supposed to be pasteurized. He decided he was not going to be worried about that.

On the way back he encountered sheep loose in the road, having made or found a gap in the fence which normally penned them in. Since there was no traffic, it did not matter. But climbing the hill into the town he met someone coming down on foot. A cracked voice greeted him by name, but it took him a moment or two to recognize Jack, the garage hand who serviced his grandfather's car. This was an old old man, ready to drop: Jack was in his middle twenties.

Neil mumbled some kind of answer. What was there to say? He had become accustomed to the terrible alteration produced by the Plague, and learned to view it with no more than a shiver of revulsion. But this time the shiver was deeper, and had fear in it. Jack was the youngest victim he had seen – by ten years at least.

The weather, which had been unsettled, stabilized into high pressure and a cloudless sky. The day after Neil's grandmother died the sun beat harshly down against the white walls of the houses, and by the middle of the afternoon it was very hot. The smell of death grew stronger. The corpse-lorry had been full the previous day; today it did not appear.

Evening brought a lessening of the heat, but it was still warm. There had been no electricity for twenty-four hours, and he guessed it would be a long time before it came back. He switched on the battery radio, and searched the air waves. There were few stations broadcasting: a couple in French, one in German, one in what was probably Dutch. Eventually he found the BBC, and a voice monotonously reciting emergency regulations and instructions. They related chiefly to life in the cities, and it was possible to read a fairly horrific picture into them. Much was made of the country being under martial law, and there were repeated warnings that troops had orders to shoot looters on sight.

Neil switched off. It was discouraging, told him nothing useful, and was a waste of precious batteries. He made himself a supper of tinned ham and baked beans; then sat staring out of the window as the dusk deepened. Someone on the other side of the road had lit candles, but that was the only light showing. He had candles of his own, but thought he would save them like the radio batteries. In the distance a dog howled for a time. After that there was a period of silence, before the din started.

It began as a distant whine, which rapidly became identifiable as the oncoming roar of motorbike engines. They were coming from the Hastings direction, and not taking the bypass road but heading into the town. The noise swelled and faded, changing note, and he guessed they were going through towards Rye. But the roar flared up again, sank and rose and went on in that pattern.

They were clearly racing round and round the church-yard square. Curiosity took Neil out of doors and along the dark street to look. Headlights flashed in front of him, and he ducked out of sight into a doorway.

There were half a dozen, the riders leather-jacketed and wearing white helmets painted with a black device – a skull possibly. They went on roaring round the square, the reverberation of their engines hammering the night air. No-one came out from the surrounding houses, or if they did they too were keeping under cover.

After a dozen or so circuits they turned into Hiham Gardens and the engines stopped. He heard shouts and a crash of glass, and realized they were raiding the pub. It had been closed for some days, but there would be liquor there.

31

Neil stayed where he was; he had an uneasy feeling about going back to the house while they were still in the town. It was about half an hour before the engines started up, once more heading for the High Street. Again they made the circuit of the churchyard. They swept past his doorway and he heard them shouting above the blast of the engines, but could not make the words out. They were driving one-handed with bottles in their free hands.

They made two complete circuits. On the third, first the leader and then the others in turn rose in the saddle and hurled the bottles to crash high against the wall of the church. That was the end; they passed him again but turned left instead of right, and the racket retreated southwards.

When the silence had come back, Neil walked along to the east front of the church. He guessed they had been aiming the bottles at the stained glass windows, but as far as he could see in the dark they had missed.

As he went back along the quiet street, lacking even its solitary lamp at the corner of the square and lit only by the glimmer of a rising moon, he thought about the incident. They had been tearaways from Hastings presumably, on the rampage. A quiet enough rampage – they had done relatively little damage – but next time might be different, in a world where law and order was either armed soldiers or non-existent. It would make sense, he supposed, to find a place out in the country – like the farmhouse where he had milked the cow – and hive up until the Plague was over and life had become normal again. But he had a reluctance to move away from the place he knew; even the hateful smell of death, pervading everywhere, was not enough to overcome it.

He let himself into the empty house and lit a candle. He only had half a dozen: the shop had been sold out before it closed down. He decided to go into Rye the following day and try to find some.

Rye was horrifying. It was not so empty as Winchelsea: Neil saw quite a few people in the streets, and a couple of motor-cars being driven. But the people had dazed hopeless expressions and the smell of death was overpowering, a sickly cloying sweetness which hung nauseatingly on the hot breeze. He travelled the length of the High Street and paused to stare from the Lookout on Hilder's Cliff. The marsh stretched away, green and empty, traversed by a trafficless road but specked with the familiar white dots of sheep. Immediately below on the Salts were the lines of brown and one gaping ditch. Presumably it had been left like that when the bulldozer operator died or fled. He could see the whiteness of lime at the bottom of the ditch.

He had found no candles: people would have stripped the shops when they realized power supplies were likely to go. Most of the shops were closed, in fact, but a few remained open. One of these was a grocer's, and Neil traded useless pound notes for tinned foods and plastic-wrapped bacon. The shopkeeper, an anxious man in his middle years, expressed some scruples about the latter: it had been in the cellar since the refrigerator stopped working, but he could not guarantee its freshness.

Neil said: "It doesn't matter."

The shopkeeper looked at the notes he was putting in his till.

"No," he said, "I suppose it doesn't." He took off his spectacles and stared at Neil from blank eyes. "I had the fever two days ago."

Neil was anxious to leave; the town depressed him unutterably. He had come in on an old bicycle he had found abandoned in Winchelsea, and which he had left at the bottom of the Mint. On the way to get it he met someone else he knew, but this time it was he who spoke.

It was not the face he recognized – he could never have done that. But the red hair and the canary yellow waistcoat were unmistakable; worn by an old man he knew to be only months older than himself. He stopped, shocked more by this than by anything so far.

"Hendrix. . . . Is it you?"

Hendrix looked at him dully. He seemed to be about to speak; then shrugged as though the effort was too much, and shuffled on.

Neil pedalled fast out of Rye and along the empty road through the Marsh. He felt sick and out of sorts, but had a curious sense of exhilaration and lightheadedness. It was good to be in open country after the nauseating smell of the town.

The exhilaration evaporated as he pushed the bicycle up the steep hill into Winchelsea. It was replaced by a leaden feeling, not merely in his legs, but in his back and arms. He went on through the town gate and up the last few yards of incline, but reaching level ground did nothing to lessen his fatigue. At every step of the way along the last hundred yards he wanted to drop everything and curl up in the road.

The bicycle slipped as he tried to prop it against the wall of the house, and he made no attempt to pick it up. He managed to get the shopping bag with the food into the kitchen, but no more: he was too dead beat to put things away.

The mirror over the mantel in the sitting room showed him his face: cheeks flushed crimson, brow beaded with sweat. His head was beginning to ache, and he found himself shivering uncontrollably. There was a thermometer upstairs in the bathroom, but the top of the stairs might as well have been the summit of Everest. And he did not need telling that he had a high temperature: the palm of his hand burned against his forehead.

So this is what it's like, he thought; and sank, uncaring, on to the sofa.

He did not move during the rest of the day or the following night except to stumble out to the kitchen when driven by thirst. It seemed strange and wonderful that water ran from the tap; after he had drunk deeply he put his head underneath and soaked it. Then he went back and drifted into a sleep of nightmareish dreams. He was in the car again, watching the juggernaut loom in front. But there was no crash – only his parents and brother and sister staring at him from blank, wrinkled faces. And he was at school, with Hendrix jeering "London wet . . ." in a voice that cracked and faded. Dream slipped into dream, each episode more ridiculous and horrifying than the one before. Once or twice he awoke, hearing his own voice crying out and the hot silence of the night sinking back.

In the morning he did move, but only as far as his bedroom where he lay, feverish and stupefied, for the rest of the day. During the next night the fever went down. He awoke to the sound of birds – sparrows under the eaves, a thrush further off – and a feeling of ravenous hunger.

Downstairs he looked at bacon, eggs and potatoes in the larder and was momentarily dizzied by the thought of a gigantic fry-up. But the cooker was useless, of course, without power. He opened a tin of baked beans and one of tuna. It was not what he would have chosen for breakfast, but he wolfed it and felt better. A cup of tea would have improved things, but you needed power for that, too.

As he rinsed the dirty plate under the tap, he thought about it. Gas supplies had probably been cut off as well; it would have been unsafe to keep them on. Outlying places, though, might have bottled gas, or solid-fuel or oil-fired cookers.

It would be worth exploring. The reluctance he had felt about leaving the house was no longer there. The thing was to be practical, and cope with things as they were. He could try going back to the farm for a start.

While he was thinking that he caught sight of his face in an old looking glass that hung above the sink, and remembered. Not that there was anything unusual to be seen: it was the face he had seen in mirrors all his life – the same slightly squashed nose, high cheekbones, pink complexion, brown curly hair.

Neil dropped the plate and heard it clatter in the bowl. No difference showed, but there was a difference. Even though the mark was invisible he had been marked. He had had the fever. He had maybe a week to live; maybe less.

FOUR

NEIL SAW FEWER PEOPLE each day. Those he did encounter in the ghost-like streets of the little town seemed as disinclined for contact, for greeting even, as he was himself. It was funny, he thought: it had been understandable in the beginning, when people were hoping to avoid catching the Plague and shunned possible carriers. But now, surely, they must know there was no way of missing it? They were all victims, or destined soon to be. And yet he himself, knowing he had had the fever, found himself crossing the road if he saw someone coming in the opposite direction.

On the fourth day following the fever he saw no-one. His supplies were running out, and he went to the shop which had been the first to close. There was no sign of life, but he rapped on the door, loudly and repeatedly. After some time he stood back, and called:

"Is anyone in?"

His voice echoed. He called again, more loudly, then shouted:

"Is someone alive in there? Or anywhere?"

The hot weather still held, and a scent of roses mingled with the smell of death. He looked desperately around at the neat white clapboard houses. Surely someone would open a window, lean out, call? It did not matter what – a demand for silence would be enough.

But nothing came. He waited again; then picked up a stone, smashed the glass of the door, reached in and undid the bolt. It was dim inside the shop and cooler, with a smell of rotting vegetables adding to the other smells. Something moved in the shadows and he checked, startled. It was only a cat: large, tabby, glossy. It came to him, amiable and unafraid, purring and pushing its head against his leg. It did not look at all starved; either enough food had been left out for it or there was a plentiful supply of mice. Or, more likely, it could get in and out through a cat-door at the back.

At least the shelves were full of tins of food, and Neil found a cardboard box and methodically filled it. He did not bother to leave money: that was all over, too. As he left the shop, carrying his burden into the heat, the cat followed. He encouraged it, calling "Puss." He thought it might come with him but at the end of the street, perhaps with memories of traffic snarling along the High Street, it turned back.

Neil rested his box on top of the churchyard gate; he had filled it rather too full for carrying comfort. The graves stretched out in front, their stones grey among the uncut grass. The church clock had stopped at just after half past seven. He looked at his own watch and realized he had forgotten to wind it: it said a quarter to four. He wondered what time it was – somewhere around mid-day from the position of the sun in the sky. No BBC time signal, but he might find a sun-dial. He shrugged as he lifted the box and went through the gate. It didn't matter.

Several times during the afternoon he thought he heard what sounded like a human voice. He told himself it was probably no more than imagination, and in any case what did it matter? But in the end he went to investigate.

It was louder as he approached the row of houses called Trojan's Platt, a whimpering cry. Neil traced it to a particular house and nerved himself to approach, and then to call in at the window:

"Who is it? Are you all right?"

The whimpering ended. He waited, but nothing happened. Moments ticked by. It had stopped, whatever, whoever it was, and the old urge returned – to go away, avoid contact, crawl back into his hole and wait for death. He was starting to move when the front door opened.

It had taken him a long time because it had not been easy: he had had to stretch on tiptoe to reach the latch, and strain to pull it back. He looked at Neil from a dirty tear-smeared face. He was about six years old.

His name, it seemed, was Tommy – Tommy Mitcham, he said, and went on to reel off his address. His parents would have taught him to do that in case he got lost: Neil remembered his mother teaching him. She could never have imagined him being lost like this.

He told his story haltingly but clearly. Mummy and Daddy had got sick, and then died. They were upstairs. They had told him not to go out without them. He had been eating biscuits, but they were all gone. He was hungry.

Neil said: "That's all right, Tommy. I have some food. You come with me."

He hung back, standing in the doorway. Neil put his hand out.

"It's all right for you to come out now. Your mummy wouldn't mind."

The boy whispered something Neil failed to catch. He asked him to speak up, and bent towards him. The boy whispered:

"Susie."

"Susie?"

Tommy turned and went back into the house, and Neil followed him. The room was very untidy, with toys and

39

clothes and biscuit wrappings scattered everywhere. In front of the empty fireplace was a rug, cherry red, with a yellow half-moon on it and a couple of big silver stars. On the half-moon a very grubby two-year-old girl, partly dressed by her brother's fumbling fingers, lay sprawled asleep.

Tommy looked at him, expectant but doubtful. Neil said:

"That's all right. We'll take Susie with us."

Neil carried her back, with Tommy trotting beside him. She was half asleep and mumbled words he did not catch, but seemed quite happy. In the house he ran water into the bath, and put them both in. They accepted this contentedly, not minding the water being cold because the day was so hot. That solved the question of clothes, too, for the time being; after he had dried them on a bath towel he let them run about naked. The clothes they had been wearing were too filthy to be put back on.

He set about opening tins to make a meal for them and they were soon eating hungrily. While they got on with that – the little girl was more deft with a spoon than he had expected – he washed their clothes through and hung them out to dry.

Later, while they played with china figurines from his grandmother's china cabinet, he watched and thought about them. The Plague had struck first at the old, later at the middle-aged, finally at young people. Youth had offered a greater resistance to its onslaught, which seemed to suggest there might be something, some innate defence, which weakened as people grew older. And might that not mean that in the very young the defence would be strong enough to defy the Plague completely?

Susie, playing with a shepherdess with a crook and a lamb, dropped it and it smashed on the floor. Neil remembered his grandmother letting him hold that piece, very carefully, telling him it was a special piece of Dresden and extremely valuable. Susie looked alarmed, and he thought she might be about to cry. He quickly found her something else, a Limoges jug with snails crawling up the outside, to amuse her.

These two, he thought with a growing excitement, really might survive. But could they cope, small and unskilled as they were, with the day-to-day problems of living?

He went to a mirror and looked at his reflection. There was no sign of ageing yet: the lines in his face were only lines of nervousness and disappeared when he relaxed. But he could not have long. Three days? Four, at most. Not long to prepare a boy of six for the task of looking after himself and a helpless younger sister. But one must do the best with what one had. He called:

"Tommy?"

"Yes, Neil?"

"There are some things I want to show you. How to use a tin-opener, to begin with."

Neil got them to bed early. Tommy asked to be told a story, and he did what he could in the way of remembering one his father had been in the habit of telling them at bedtime, about a big steam puffer train and a little electric train. It sounded more and more ridiculous as he went on with it, but Tommy seemed to enjoy it, laughing at places where he remembered laughing, and asking questions he was hard put to answer. Susie made no contribution but sucked a thumb contentedly, staring up at the ceiling.

They wanted to be kissed goodnight, or Tommy at least, and he did that and tucked them in. Then he went downstairs, and thought about ways of helping them to survive.

Food and shelter were the fundamentals. Tommy had been very good at picking up the use of the tin-opener: fortunately it was of a kind that was relatively easy to operate. He must get in a really big stock of tinned foods; or

41

perhaps take Tommy along to the shop and show him how to forage for himself. Then clothes. They obviously could not manage with the ones he had washed, even in the summer. There was no clothes shop in Winchelsea. He could go into Rye, but it would be easier and made more sense for him to go back to Trojan's Platt. He did not much fancy venturing upstairs into the presence of the dead parents, even though he had grown used to death and corpses, but there would be clothes there to fit them, though probably nothing that would be of much value for the winter. They would have outgrown last year's and next year's would not yet have been bought.

Thinking of that he felt a sudden quick despair. What chance was there, in reality? They might survive the summer months if he left them a large enough supply of food, but how could they possibly cope with winter? If they did not starve, the cold would finish them off.

Neil shook his head. It was hopeless, but he would not abandon hope. From what he had seen in this brief acquaintance he judged Tommy to be a bright boy, capable beyond his actual years. Providing they could get through the winter, spring would find Tommy nearly a year older and that much more resourceful. And Susie would be big enough to travel with him, as long as they went by easy stages. They would find more food that way: there must be large stocks in Rye and even more in Hastings.

Neil went back to the looking glass above the mantel. The sun had gone down and the room was shadowy, but he was fairly sure there was still no change. That meant little: the deterioration, when it did come, was often rapid. Three more days of usefulness? He stared into the glass, no longer seeing himself but thinking hard.

For a start, this place was no good. Water still flowed from the taps but there was no knowing how long that would last; and although he could open up the old town well and show Tommy, using it would be too difficult and dangerous for a child. And it was too far from an adequate

42

food source. No, it would have to be somewhere else – somewhere with a spring or stream close by and to which, in the short time remaining, he could bring the essentials to keep them alive.

He felt relaxed; more at peace than he had been for a long time. He went into the bedroom where the little ones were and found them both asleep, with their covers kicked off. He replaced them, and Tommy mumbled something without waking up.

Looking down at them, he wondered what the odds were. A hundred to one against, or a thousand? Worth taking, anyway. And first things first: he would go and get clothes for them.

Neil was up soon after six. Sunshine slanted in at his window, promising another fine day. He found Susie sitting up; she smiled as he came into the room. He woke Tommy, and set him to the task of washing and dressing himself and his sister.

After they had breakfasted, off corned beef and biscuits, he explained to Tommy that he had to leave them for the day. The boy looked unhappy, and he explained that he would be looking for a better place for them to live in. Tommy accepted that, but wanted to come with him. Neil told him he was needed to stay and look after Susie. He did not argue with that, but said:

"You will come back, Neil, won't you?"

Neil had scrutinized his morning face. He said with confidence:

"Don't worry. I'll come back."

He had worked out the requirements with some care. An adequate water supply and reasonable proximity to supplies of tinned food were the basic needs; beyond that it was a question of settling for the best that was offered, bearing in mind that he could not afford to spend too much time on the quest. The countryside just outside Rye offered the most promising scope, and he got on his bicycle

43

and pedalled down the hill in that direction.

He searched throughout the morning with no success. Once his hopes were raised by finding a farmhouse with a pump-handle in the kitchen, but closer inspection showed it had been kept for ornamental purposes only: the handle yielded to the pressure of his arm but nothing happened. Apart from mains supplies the nearest water was several hundred yards away, in the form of a stagnant pool.

That was around noon. He was hot and tired and hungry. He found a ham in the larder – the larder was north-facing, cool, and the ham smelt all right – and cut thick slices which he ate ravenously. He had not gone upstairs but took it for granted now that there would be no-one left alive. He had seen plenty of animals: sheep, stray dogs and cats, and a horse, saddled and bridled, that snorted at him before trotting away; but nothing human.

Some sense of discouragement was inevitable, but he refused to give way to it. He washed down the ham with a bottle of cider, and set off again. This felt like the hottest day so far, and his bicycle wheels ploughed through patches of melting tar. He had stripped off his shirt and tied it around his waist, but after a time resumed wearing it. He could not risk sunburn, with all that had to be done.

In mid-afternoon he found it, and could not believe his luck. It was a sprawling timbered farmhouse, parts of it probably Elizabethan, and a stream ran alongside. The stream was narrow but fiercely flowing, and sheltered by the house's southern wall. It would run even in a deep frost.

The sitting room had an open fireplace, and logs were stacked in the yard outside – a huge pile reaching up to the eaves. They were of a size a child could handle, and he could break down the pile to enable Tommy to get at them more easily. With matches and a supply of firelighters, they should be able to keep warm. Plus a stern lesson in fire precautions. There was a risk, but it was better than leaving them at the mercy of the winter.

It was situated less than a mile from Rye: the sitting room window framed a view of red roofs and the church with its weathercock glinting in the sunlight. Tomorrow he could bring them over, and start moving in supplies. But to save precious time he could make a beginning of that part of the operation right away.

In Rye the smell was worse than ever, and he had to force himself through a miasma that almost seemed to drag physically at his limbs. The heat was making things worse, but he took consolation from the fact that it was accelerating the inevitable process of decay. It would not be long before it was over: there would be only clean bones in the world Tommy and Susie went out to explore.

The town was quite deserted. Neil wondered about small children: if Tommy and Susie had survived there ought to be many others in a place as big as this. But those big enough to do so would have fled, he guessed, from this charnel-house, and the rest would not have survived. He did stop to listen once or twice for crying, but was guiltily relieved when he heard nothing. He had a commitment already, and Tommy would have enough to do in caring for his sister.

In an ironmonger's shop he found a galvanized iron wheelbarrow with pneumatic tyres. He went into a chain grocers, broke into a store room at the rear, and was surrounded by aisles of plenty. He filled the wheelbarrow too full at first, and had to shed part of the load to make it manageable. It was an advantage that Rye, like Winchelsea, stood on a hill, making the descent to the farmhouse relatively easy.

He made four trips before he decided to call it a day. He had the beginnings of a stockpile, and even if he woke up changed in the morning and was too feeble to do much more in the way of fetching, he could show Tommy where to go. He was very tired, but contented.

There was one more thing needed doing in the house. He went upstairs for the first time and looked at what was there: three bodies in all, two in one room and the third in another. He steeled himself to pull that one off the bed and drag it in its sheet along the landing and into the room with the others. Even had he been able to bear it, he could not spare the time burial would have required. The bedroom had a key: he turned it behind him and went downstairs. Before mounting his bicycle, he threw the key far off into a shrubbery.

Neil had a moment's apprehension as he pushed the bicycle up the last bit of the hill, under the stone gateway, that he might not find them there – that they might have wandered away during his absence. But Susie appeared in the hallway, answering his call and stumbling towards him with her rolling infant's gait. He picked her up and carried her through, calling Tommy, who answered from the garden.

There was something odd in his voice and Neil wondered if he might be getting a summer cold. He would need to add a few basic medicaments to the farmhouse store, and advice on using them. Tommy came in, walking slowly as though he were tired, but he reminded himself it had been a long day, involving some strenuous playing probably. He put Susie down, despite her protests, and went to greet the boy.

He stopped some feet away, struggling not to show his incredulity and horror. A little old man stared at him from the face of a child.

Neil had a feeling of revulsion which it was not easy to master, but he managed – holding the ageing boy in his arms, kissing him at bedtime. Tommy had no idea of what was happening, and there was a chance, Neil thought, that he need not do so during the time remaining. He made an excuse to put them in separate rooms, in case Susie revealed something in her baby-talk, and went round the house hiding mirrors. The ones above the dressing tables he dismantled, and he locked the room which had the wardrobe with a full-length mirror in the door.

The precautions were unnecessary. In the morning Tommy said he was tired, and it was no problem to persuade him to stay in bed. Susie, on the other hand, was full of energy, and he took her downstairs to give her breakfast. He had no appetite himself, and sat watching her and trying to behave normally as she chattered away.

"Where Tommy?" she demanded at one point.

Neil said:"Tommy's not very well. He's staying in bed this morning."

She nodded, accepting it as natural, and reached for another biscuit. Her face glowed with health and her thick blonde hair was tangled, despite his having brushed and combed it less than half an hour before. Although he had reconciled himself to what had happened to Tommy, he could not believe she would suffer the same fate. But if not, what difference did it make? Tommy might have had a chance of surviving in a world empty of people. For Susie there was none: she would perish within days of his protection being removed.

It was almost with relief that he heard her complain, in mid-afternoon, of being tired, and subsequently saw the chubby face starting to lose its pinkness, drying and wrinkling. He put her to bed early, and she did not object. In the other bedroom he found Tommy awake, but very feeble. He asked in a cracked whisper for a drink of water, and Neil brought him a glass and held it to his lips: his arms were too weak to support it.

Tommy whispered again:"You won't go away, Neil?"

He shook his head. "I won't go away."

Neil slept that night on a mattress which he dragged through to the landing and positioned between the opened doors of their two bedrooms. He was awake a good deal during the night and a couple of times looked in on them. The second time Tommy was lying still; he touched his

47

face and found it cold.

Susie slept through most of the day, and went peacefully towards evening. Neil had spent part of the afternoon digging a trench close to the grave of his grandparents. It was an easier task than the other, being so much shorter.

It was easy, too, with dusk coming on, to carry out the two small bodies, wrapped in sheets, and lay them side by side in the grave. He felt very tired as he pushed earth over them with the spade. He thought it was probably happening to him as well, and was numbly contented. He went in, washed, ate sparingly, and lay down on his bed. The house was empty, but so was the town, the world. It might be he was the last person alive on earth. He was glad, as sleep took him, that it would not be for long.

For a week after that he lived like an automaton: eating, drinking, sleeping, trying not to think and for the most part succeeding. He did not bother to look at himself, and since he had put away the mirrors did not happen on his reflection accidentally. He had a dim feeling that it was taking too long, but all his thoughts were slack and dull and he did not pursue it.

The weather had finally broken and the days were dark and stormy, with wind and rain howling and hammering along the street outside. The wind was violent at times, and once he heard a pane of glass break somewhere at the back of the house, but did not bother to go and look. It did not matter. Nothing mattered.

One morning, though, the sun came out again, and he saw his shadowy image on the white side of the refrigerator. He put a hand to his face and felt his cheeks, full and unlined. It was a fortnight since he had had the fever.

It took several more days for him to be sure he had somehow escaped the fate that had overtaken everyone else. That was when he left the house for the first time since the children died. He thought, with a new sense of misery, of his grandfather's remarks about his will, and the inheritance that was to come to him. A good education, a decent profession. . . . He had a bigger inheritance than that: a vacated planet.

His steps took him, without particular intent, to the church. He stood inside it and looked round at the old stone walls, the effigies of knights in their niches. What was the name for the celebration of thanksgiving – the Te Deum? The walls must have echoed to scores, hundreds of those, over the centuries.

He thought of the tearaways on their motorbikes, trying to break the windows with their bottles. All dead now. He found a silver candle-stick, hefted it, swung his arm and threw. The first two shots were ineffective, the candle-stick crashing against stone and falling. But the third went home and he heard the crash of glass. The candle-stick did not fall that time, but remained wedged in the leads. It stuck close by an apostle's hand; as though he were carrying it to bed, but upside down.

He stayed there a long time before going out from the quiet of the church to the world's quiet.

FIVE

THE RATS drove Neil out of Winchelsea.

He had no idea how long he stayed on after the children died: time meant nothing, and day followed day on a treadmill of sunrise and sunset, light and darkness, rain and shine.

He stayed in his grandparents' house, but developed a habit of going into other houses in the town. He preferred those that had family pictures on show, because they helped to people the emptiness. One day he found himself talking to a photograph of a motherly-looking woman, as though it were a real person. He broke off on the realization, and did not go back there.

The animals became wilder. He saw the glossy tabby that had followed him from the shop; it was leaner now, watched him suspiciously from the top of a wall, and leapt away on the other side when he called to it. The dogs for the most part had collected in packs. They gave Neil a wide berth. He was not sorry about this because they had a formidable look, and a fight between two of the packs kept him awake one night and left blood stains and patches of hair in the street next morning.

50

One dog, a Labrador cross, approached him, and seemed half-inclined to allow itself to be adopted. He gave it food and water but it did not stay, and a couple of days later he saw it running with one of the packs. His encouragement of it, he thought, had probably been half-hearted. He had liked the dog and would not have minded keeping it, but it did not offer him anything he much wanted. The empty rooms with the family photographs were better in that respect.

Flies became a nuisance. Whenever it was at all warm they swarmed, bloated and buzzing, impudent beyond belief in their attacks on anything that moved. He knew what had brought about this population explosion, but shut his mind to it as far as possible. In one of the shops he found a stack of aerosol sprays, and was able to keep the rooms he used free of their pestering. Outside it was different. A cow wandered into the town one day, its face black with them, the eyes in particular. It went off at quite a gallop when Neil approached it. The udders swung slack and empty, showing she had gone out of milk.

The rats followed the flies, and were worse. He only had glimpses of them at first – a brown body slinking along a gutter or running across the street with its hideous hump-backed scuttering motion. But they rapidly multiplied and grew more daring. He understood the reason for their multiplication, too, and this time could not blank it out.

That by itself would not have been enough to impel him to move: the sense of revulsion was less strong than the feeling of inertia, of reluctance to do anything beyond the routine, which had held him since he found himself alone. But the rats went on increasing and began to appear in packs like the dogs, and by day, indifferent to other living things. Or at first indifferent. One day he saw one of the dogs, a small ill-looking brown mongrel, limping in the rear after its companions had run down the High Street. The rats seemed to come from nowhere, a darker brown stream made up of hundreds of living hungry bodies, and the dog went down, yelping in agony. Neil was some fifty yards from the scene. There was nothing to be done, and he turned away back to the house. The yelping did not last long.

He thought about it in the sitting room, in front of the blank screen of the television set. His supply of biscuits had run out some days before, and when he had gone to the shop he had found only gnawed scraps of paper where there had been a shelf of wrapped packets. The rats were running out of food, too. Eventually cannibalism would restore a balance, but until that time they would be an increasing menace. They would pull down more than a puny terrier before they turned on one another.

He left early the following morning, taking only a change of clothes in a haversack. He cycled in the direction of Rye, but did not enter the town: the rat situation there was likely to be worse than in Winchelsea. He went instead to the farmhouse he had intended as a refuge for Tommy and Susie.

It was a day of cloud and sunshine, warm after rain. Neil propped his bicycle against a wall and went into the kitchen. It was just the same, with the supplies of food piled in the cupboards as he had left them. There was enough to last him a long time – a month at least. Looking at them he had a piercing recollection of the way he had felt that afternoon: the sense of achievement, the hope for a future which, even though he would not share it, was worth planning and labouring for.

He thought of Tommy and Susie and began to cry; sniffling at first, then miserably and helplessly. It was the first time he had wept since the car smash.

Gradually during the weeks that followed he started to come alive again. It was a slow process, broken by relapses into numbness and lethargy. Once he stayed in bed for two days, only moving to get a snack or go to the bathroom. But a change was taking place. He felt his mind moving out of the fog in which for so long it had been lost.

One day, in the course of another heatwave, Rye caught fire. A pall of black smoke hung over it by day and flames lit the night sky. It was inevitable, he realized, as small fires, accidentally started by something like the sun's rays beaming through glass, spread for want of human control. In a place like Rye, close-packed with mainly wooden houses, a conflagration was certain; it was only surprising it hadn't happened sooner. It offered an interesting spectacle, but no more than that. You could not even think of it as a town burning: a town, by definition, had inhabitants.

Watching it he found himself speculating on human existence – its purpose, if it had a purpose. He thought about God, at first with a kind of contemptuous anger at someone who, if not the actual author of what had happened, had permitted it at least, observing with a cold eternal eye as his creatures, good and bad together, perished and rotted.

From this he passed to the contemplation of his own survival. What was he that he should have been spared, to live in a desert world? He searched his self for anything which might merit so terrible a favour, and could discover nothing.

But what if it were no favour, but a punishment? Perhaps it was wickedness which had caused him to be singled out. Perhaps even – the thought struck him with a savagery that made his head reel – none of this had really happened; he had been killed with the others in the car smash and this was a nightmare, some kind of purgatory. . . .

The notion tormented him for a time until other considerations replaced it. He felt the pangs of hunger and realized that in watching the fire he had forgotten his evening meal. Appetite, the awareness of a body requiring nourishment, demonstrated the absurdity of the fancy, and he went to the kitchen to get a tin of stew.

He kept the fire in the sitting room going most of the

time; he had found a trivet and rigged up an arrangement for cooking over it. As he sat in front of the saucepan where the stew was heating, the whole line of speculation which had engaged him seemed to lose its substance. Before any of this happened he had regarded himself as an agnostic. What had occurred since, however terrible, was not a reason for inventing either a punishing or a rewarding God.

It had happened, and that was that. He was alone in the world and must make the best of it.

Yet his mind was quite wakened now. Curiosity of a more ordinary kind suddenly beckoned. An empty world, and his, to do with it what he liked. The need he had felt to hide away, to cling to a small security, gave way to its opposite. There was a planet outside to explore.

As soon as he had decided, he was eager to be off. London, and the possibilities it offered, seized his imagination, but there was the problem of getting there. How far – seventy miles? He did not fancy walking, nor bicycling for that matter; and even if he could catch a horse he doubted his ability to master the riding of it. A motor car, though. . . . He was no longer disbarred by age, or the need to pass a driving test. And it was not the Queen's highway any more, but his.

The garage attached to the farmhouse held two cars – a new Rover automatic and a battered Mini. He found the ignition keys for both on a nail in the hall, and tried them out. He preferred the Rover, not because it was bigger and glossier but on the assumption that an automatic car would be easier to drive, and was pleased to find the instruction booklet in the glove compartment. He studied the instructions, adjusted the seat, and attempted to drive it out of the garage. The starter motor whirred, but nothing else happened. He tried several times before it occurred to him to look at the fuel gauge. It showed empty; what little petrol might have been left in the tank had clearly evaporated.

The Mini's gauge, on the other hand, registered half full. There was no booklet, but he did his best to recall what he had seen his father do. The engine roared into life, the din reverberating from the garage walls, and Neil pushed the gear lever into first and gingerly took his foot off the clutch pedal. The car bounded forward a few inches, and the engine stalled.

This process, of starting and bucking to a halt, happened a few more times and eventually the car was halfway out of the garage. At that point it refused to start at all. He went on twisting the key with no more success, and was feeling like getting out of the car and kicking it when he noticed the choke knob still extended and realized he had probably flooded the carburettor. That, too, was something remembered from his father; along with the knowledge that the only thing to do was wait for it to dry out.

A quarter of an hour later he tried again, and on his second attempt managed to get the car into gear and crawling across the yard. Fortunately it was very large and gave him room to manoeuvre. He drove round, mastering the steering and developing a growing sense of satisfaction which was lost the moment he tried to change up into second gear. The Mini stalled, and went on stalling whenever he attempted the operation.

He was impatient to go, and reflected that even in bottom gear he could travel a good deal faster than on a bicycle, and in more comfort. He collected the few things he wanted, threw them in the back, and set off along the bumpy lane leading to the main road. Smoke still hung over Rye but much less densely: the fire had largely burnt itself out. Anyway, he was not going that way.

He took the Winchelsea bypass rather than go through the town. At the foot of the hill on the far side he felt sufficiently confident to have another go at changing gears, and with a certain amount of grinding actually got into top. He was pleased with himself until he attempted to change down on the approach to Icklesham, and came to an ignoble halt.

Re-starting, he crawled on in low gear. The outskirts of Hastings surrounded him with neat modern houses, stretching away in rows. He had a feeling that there must be someone living, behind all those doors and windows — that at any moment the sound of the Mini's approach would bring a figure out, waving, into the road. But nothing moved; and rounding a bend he came on the scene of an accident, with a big transporter truck pinning down a small saloon car. Skeletons manned both rusting wrecks, shattering the illusion. The wreckage took up most of the road; there was barely room to get the Mini through.

He did not go right into Hastings but took the road north. He had started late in the afternoon and by the time he got to Robertsbridge, at his slow rate of travel, the sun was behind the houses. He noticed that the fuel gauge was now on the quarter mark, and wondered what that indicated in the way of petrol. The road map he had taken from the Rover showed Lamberhurst as the nearest town, quite a long way north. He didn't relish the thought of being stranded for the night by an empty tank, out on the open road.

Self-Service was signposted at a filling station, and he pulled in there and tried to work the pump. There was no result and he realized he had been a fool to think there could be, since the mechanism would be electrical. The solution, he worked out, was to swap the Mini in favour of a car with a fuller tank. There were several in the fore-court, but none with an ignition key. He drove on, and stopped again beside a pub. It would be better to spend the night here, and find a car in the morning.

He had brought some food with him, but did not need it. In the kitchen of the pub there was a deep freeze, which he was careful not to open, but a stock of tinned foods as well; and in the bar he found two tins of potato crisps packets, and racks holding bags of nuts and cheese biscuits. He spent the night on a huge imitation leather settee in the lounge, with a curtain to cover him. He had seen no rats, and thought the menace might be over, but he was careful about securing doors and windows before he settled down.

Neil had a bath next morning in the guest bathroom, a spacious white-tiled room with lozenges of stained glass set in the window and a long Edwardian bath raised on a dais and approached by a couple of wooden steps. Although the morning was quite warm, he shivered a little as he washed himself; at the farmhouse he had been in the habit of taking the chill off with a kettle of boiling water.

Later, he hunted through the town for another car. Most he examined were lacking an ignition key, and where he did find one the petrol tanks were either empty or too low to be worth the risk of setting out. A couple of cars had both key and petrol, but would not start. Those two stood out in the open, and he discovered their batteries had dried out in the summer heat. He concentrated after that on garaged cars, which had been protected from the sun.

When his luck turned, it turned properly: a Jaguar XJ automatic, looking as though it had just been driven from the showroom, and in fact with less than 2,000 on the clock. Neil climbed in gingerly, awed by the splendour, and found keys in place and a fuel gauge registering nearly full.

He was almost afraid of driving it, and studied the controls a long time before making the attempt. Despite that he was taken by surprise by the automatic drive, and dented a wing getting out of the garage. He was angry with himself. There was no-one to criticize or blame him, but he felt bad about damaging so beautiful a machine. On the road, though, his annoyance evaporated in the pleasure of driving. The smoothness of it was amazing after the Mini, and there was the exhilaration of speed when he got on to the open road. A squall of rain blew up, and he pressed buttons in search of the wipers. The first he tried filled the air with music from a cassette player. It was not entirely to his taste – a classical symphony – but after so long hearing only the sounds of nature it seemed like magic.

He drove on through the morning, and was in the outer London suburbs before he halted. It was a shopping centre, transfixed in a Sunday morning that would never end. The blank fronts showed fading signs – Four Hour Cleaning . . . This Week's Special Offer . . . Frying To-night. . . .

That one was a fish-and-chip shop, and out of curiosity, Neil went inside. Someone had gone through a familiar routine of preparations, before crawling away to die. There was oil in the vats, a tray containing a dried-up pulp that still smelt fishy, a bucket full of the withered remains of chipped potatoes. He prowled on, and in a back room found sacks of potatoes, somewhat soft and wrinkled, but apparently edible. He could not work the burners in the shop, but he should be able to find an open hearth somewhere and make a wood fire. He stuffed potatoes into his anorak pockets, and filled an empty milk bottle with oil; but after sniffing poured it back. It smelt rancid, and there would be no difficulty in finding more. This was a land of plenty, after all.

He made his fire in the back parlour of a shop nearby, where he also found a frying pan, an unopened bottle of corn oil, and a tin of sausages which he fried up with the potatoes. The result was greasy and not particularly nice, but it filled his belly.

When he went out again he looked over to where he had parked the Jaguar, not very neatly, in the road opposite. It had rained while he was making the meal, and the wind-screen was covered with raindrops which dazzled in the renewed sunlight. He could see the interior only indistinctly, but he had a crazy impression of someone sitting behind the wheel.

It would vanish as he approached, he thought; but it didn't. A figure, hunched and motionless. . . . He felt a hot prickle in his scalp, and the even crazier thought that it was the owner, come back from death to reproach him for the dented wing. He hesitated; then walked forward.

The figure was real. The window, which he had left closed, was wound down. When he was within a couple of yards, a voice spoke.

"Nice wheels you've got here."

SIX

THE SOUND OF A HUMAN VOICE was even stranger and more startling than the music from the cassette player had been. As though in comment on that, the figure leaned forward and switched the player on. He listened briefly, before turning it off.

"Dullsville," he said. "But you expect that with Jags. Either Beethoven or Frank Sinatra. I picked up a load of really great stuff last week – Oscar Peterson, Mugsy Spanier, Art Tatum. But that was from an Aston-Martin."

Neil stared, trying to take it in. He said hesitantly:

"I thought. . . ."

"You were the only one left?" The other looked up, grinning. "So did I, to begin with. And there aren't many. I've been around, and I can tell you."

He was about Neil's age; within a year or eighteen months, anyway. He was smaller, but looked older. He had a thin pale face, very black hair sleeked back, and heavy gold spectacles which had, Neil realized with surprise, no lenses. He wore expensive-looking clothes – pale blue slacks and a white polo neck silk shirt, and had a gold chain round his neck. He went on:

60

"Saw the smoke from a fire, and then this little number sitting waiting. She wasn't here the last time I came through, couple of days since. So I thought I'd hang about. OK?"

He clicked open the door and stepped out. He was a couple of inches shorter than Neil, and looked frail. He put out a hand, and Neil saw that every finger carried at least one ring, some as many as three. Diamonds winked in the sunlight.

"Clive D'Arcy," he said. "Viscount D'Arcy, that is. My old man was the Earl of Blenheim. But call me Clive."

The hand was warm, under the rings. This was what it felt like, Neil remembered, to touch human flesh. He said:

"I'm Neil. Neil Miller."

Clive put a friendly hand on his arm. "Great, Neil. Come and let me show you my heap. I'm parked just round the corner."

He chatted as they walked – something about a castle, ancestral estates, horses. He'd had to let them out, to run loose. Prize bloodstock, every one an Arab . . . but what could you do without grooms? Neil listened in silence, dazed. What was momentous to him seemed to mean little or nothing to the boy at his side. But he had said there were others; it was not a first meeting for him. He was on the point of asking him about that, when Clive stopped, grasping his arm again.

"There she is. What do you think?"

Neil saw the caravan first, a long luxurious vehicle with curtained windows, gleaming white except for its silvery chrome. His gaze went to the car to which it was attached. It gleamed as brightly, but black instead of white – unmistakeably a Rolls.

Clive produced a key-ring and unlocked the door of the caravan. He went in, beckoning Neil to follow.

"Come aboard. Rest the feet. Feel like a cup of tea? Orange Pekoe, Lapsang-Souchong, or Tetley teabags? Or how about coffee? Just renewed my Rombouts yesterday."

They were in a compact kitchen, with a Calor gas cooker and refrigerator, and stainless steel sink. Clive opened a cupboard and took out a tin of ground coffee.

"Or would you sooner have Blue Mountain beans." He gestured to a gadget beside the cooker. "That's the grinder. No power problems. She carries a nice little generator. So does Bessie, of course."

"Bessie?" Neil asked helplessly.

"The Rolls. Bonny Black Bess. No, I think we'll have the Rombouts – it's quicker."

He poured water from the tap into a percolator, added coffee, lit one of the rings with a gas-lighter, and set the percolator on it. Neil was looking around. Although it was so evidently a kitchen there were puzzling additions: a stand-up mirror with a heavy silver surround that looked antique, an old-fashioned goblet on the draining board with the soft sheen of gold, a cross on the wall, outlined with what seemed like rubies.

The black eyes, deep-set in the pale face, missed nothing. Clive said:

"Pretty, aren't they? But wait till you see the real stuff." He opened another cupboard. "We'll use the Royal Doulton. I've got proper coffee cups – Sèvres – but they're not big enough for a decent drink."

Neil asked: "Where did you get it all?"

Clive shrugged. "Just bits and pieces, salvaged from the ancestral home. They weren't kept in a caravan in the old days, of course. Let me show you round, while the coffee's brewing."

There was a shower next to the kitchen, and a toilet beyond. The water tank was in the roof, Clive explained. He kept a couple of spare Calor gas cylinders for the heating, and knew where to get as many more as he wanted.

Opposite the toilet units were cupboards. Clive carelessly pulled open a door, to reveal a large quantity of

62

clothes, among which Neil saw two evening suits and a camel-hair overcoat with a fur collar. A drawer which he opened held a pile of silk shirts. In a smaller compartment to one side were several sets of cuff-links, all of gold, some jewelled as well. A rack at the bottom held shoes – black, brown and suede – and a pair of long riding boots. Another rack at the top had dozens of silk ties.

"My wardrobe," Clive said in explanation. "And this is the salon."

A door slid to one side, showing a room partitioned about a third of the way along. The smaller section, as Clive demonstrated, had a pull-out table of polished oak.

"There was a set of stackable stools, as well," he said, "but I threw them out." He indicated a pair of upright chairs against the facing wall. "Chippendale, those."

The main section had pull-out beds on either side, but because of the furniture only one lot could be used. There was a black and gilt writing desk with swelling gilt legs ending in claw-and-ball feet, a small table, intricately inlaid with marquetry, carrying a large portable cassette recorder, and a very big club armchair in green leather. A carpet on the floor glowed dully in reds and blues and amber.

"Persian," Clive explained.

That was far from being all. Built-in shelves were crammed with all kinds of treasures. Neil saw various silver and gold vessels, a set of gold and silver chessmen, an ostrich egg mounted on a golden base, a gold and ivory carving of three Chinamen fishing beside a silver pool. . . . On one wall was hung a curved sword in a gilded scabbard, and on another an ornately decorated shot-gun with a chased-silver butt. There were paintings, too: very little blank space showed at all. Clive pointed to one.

"Rembrandt. I could only bring the smaller canvases, of course."

Neil said, with a feeling of inadequacy:

"It's amazing."

"Not bad." Clive nodded with approval. "I think that's the sound of the coffee percolating."

The coffee, with Coffeemate in place of cream, was very good. As they drank it, Neil tried to find out about Clive's recent experiences but did not get far. The answers to the questions he put were vague. He had been travelling around – here and there. One place was like another. Survivors? Yes, he'd seen three or four. What ages, Neil asked? Clive shrugged: different ages. Any adults? He shook his head: they'd all been younger than himself. But hadn't he thought of joining up with them? Clive looked surprised. He was all right on his own, he said. The caravan didn't have room for more than one – not for comfortable living, at any rate.

He was rather more forthcoming when asked about supplies. He had all that very well organized, he claimed. He had found a place that had been the main supply depot for a chain of supermarkets: everything you could possibly want, and enough to last a lifetime. He only smiled knowingly, though, when Neil asked him where.

He had good access to petrol, too. He kept the boot of the Rolls full of cans, which gave him a range of seven or eight hundred miles, even at twelve miles to the gallon. He had two spare sets of tyres put by, and chains for the winter.

Although he was obviously proud of his personal provisions for the future, when Neil started talking in more general terms of what things might be like in a world stripped of all but a handful of people, Clive's interest slackened again. He was similarly uninterested when Neil talked about the Plague. Neil pointed out that the resistance-factor, whatever it was, that had been responsible for their survival was obviously age-dependent. The younger you were, the more chance you had. On the other hand, below a certain age the survivor would not have been able to cope with the basic problems of living. You needed to be young, but old enough to look after yourself.

Clive nodded indifferently. "I saw one kid about three or four."

"What happened to him?" Clive shrugged. "You didn't bring him with you?"

Clive took off the lensless gold spectacles and twirled them. Instead of replying, he said:

"Something I forgot to show you. Come see."

He led the way back to the smaller living room. There was a wooden box in one corner, something like an Armada chest, secured with an iron clasp and a heavy lock. Clive produced a key, unlocked it and lifted the lid.

"What do you think of this little lot?"

It was like something out of a corny pirate film. The chest was heaped with jewels: necklaces, armbands, tiaras, brooches, with all kinds of precious stones in elaborate gold settings. A snowy heap in one corner must have comprised a dozen strings of pearls at least. Clive picked up a black cloth bag and undid a string at the top. He held it open for Neil to look in. There were at least a hundred rings there, each with one or more big diamonds.

Comment was clearly required. Neil said:

"You brought the family jewels with you, then?"

Clive gave him a quick look; then nodded.

"That's right." He retied the bag and put it away carefully. "You bring any?"

"Only a ring of my mother's."

"Can I see it?"

Neil fished out the opal ring from his anorak pocket, and Clive looked at it.

"Pretty," he said condescendingly as he handed it back. He shut and locked his chest, and stowed away the key.

The charitable explanation was that he was mad; though whether he had been like that originally or recent events had unhinged him there was no way of knowing. His present life, certainly, owed more to fantasy than reality. The trace of cockney accent, increasingly noticeable

65

as time passed, did not fit with being Viscount D'Arcy. For that matter, could there have been an Earl of Blenheim? It had been the name of a house, surely – the Duke of Marlborough's?

All the things here, like the caravan itself and the Rolls, were items he had acquired, jackdaw-like, in his travels. Neil had been surprised that he showed such slight interest in other survivors, and shocked that he had left a four-year-old to fend for himself. But he realized that as far as Clive was concerned other people scarcely existed. His own role was merely to be shown the treasures – to serve as a mirror for greed and vanity.

That being so, there was no point, even if they were the only two people left, in attempting to extend the acquaintanceship. The slight distaste which he had felt for Clive from the start hardened into antipathy. The sooner they separated and he went his own way, the better. And the fact that there might be others still alive added weight to that.

Clive, he reckoned, ought to be equally glad to see him go. He had performed the function required; and with the appetite for display satisfied, other considerations were likely to come to the fore. He doubted if Clive could be at ease with a stranger in such close proximity to his possessions. His mania for locking things up was testimony to that.

But, again to his surprise, Clive demurred when he thanked him for the coffee and talked of moving on. He put a hand on Neil's arm, and said warmly:

"You can't go just yet. I want you to stay and have supper with me. I've got a tin of pheasant in Burgundy sauce. And a château-bottled claret to go with it."

Neil had conflicting impulses, the main one being to insist on leaving. On the other hand, this was the first human being he had seen in what seemed like an age. And though mad, he appeared harmless. It was even possible that having someone to talk to might start him back on the

66

road to sanity. He nodded.

"All right. Thanks."

There were moments during the remainder of the day when Neil thought his guess about Clive's mental state, and the possibility of it improving, had been right. A lot of what he said was obvious nonsense – he talked of hunt balls, riding to hounds, holidays in the West Indies and Africa and the United States, even of going to dinner with the Queen – but there were saner passages.

One came after he had asked Neil about his family – had he had brothers and sisters? Neil said yes, and gave their names when asked, but said nothing of their being killed before the Plague started. Clive said:

"I had three sisters. They were older than me. Jenny, Caroline and Paula. Jenny was a secretary, in a bank." He paused. "She was going to leave this summer, to get married."

Not Lady Jenny, Lady Caroline, Lady Paula, Neil noticed. And although it was not impossible for an Earl's eldest daughter to be a secretary in a bank, he would have expected Clive to invent some more elevated occupation for her. This was genuine.

He asked about them, and Clive talked at some length. Neil got the impression of a little brother indulged, spoiled in fact, by three adoring elder sisters. The parents were shadowy creatures, who seemed to have had much less importance in his life. He said:

"It got Caroline first, then Paula. I thought maybe it had missed Jenny. Then I watched it happen to her." There was a tremor in his voice. "I saw it all, from beginning to end."

He stopped abruptly, and Neil saw the dark eyes glisten. He said:

"It's over now."

He realized the inadequacy of that, but could think of nothing else to say. Clive did not speak for a moment or two; then said with exaggerated cheerfulness:

"Say, I knew there was something else I had to show you!"

He brought it from a shelf: an old book, calf-bound, with silver corners and a silver clasp.

"Look at this!"

Neil was getting bored with that cry of triumph. Clive undid the clasp and opened up the book. The pages were of yellowed parchment, lettered and coloured by hand. The text was in Latin, the script not easy to make out, but Neil realized it was religious, perhaps a bible.

"I don't go for books much," Clive said, "but this one's got some great pictures."

He turned the pages and displayed a picture of an odd-looking ship, with even odder animals staring in pairs across the high gunnels: giraffes, elephants, lions, a couple of woolly sheep. Sea and sky were different blues, both sharp and bright, and the sun was a disk of real gold leaf.

"Noah's Ark," Clive said. "I like that. I really do."

That evening, while they ate together, the talk was wild again. He had not only gone to dinner with the Queen, but stayed with her as a house-guest. It wasn't easy to work out if this had been at Buckingham Palace, Windsor Castle or Balmoral – perhaps all three. He spoke of the Royal Family as though they were old friends.

"I've been thinking about the Crown Jewels," he said. "Maybe I ought to go to the Tower and get them. For safe keeping. Her Majesty would have wanted me to do that."

At least the food was good. With the pheasant he served potatoes, asparagus and peas, and afterwards produced a tin containing a rich fruit cake. They drank the wine out of silver goblets. It had a slightly sour taste which Neil did not care much for, and he refused a refill, but Clive drank a good deal. One of the best wines from his father's cellar, he proclaimed, ignoring the fragment of label which had carried the wine merchant's price tag. They finished off with coffee – the Blue Mountain this time – and Clive told a rambling tale about his father taking the family to Switzerland: they had occupied the entire top floor of the biggest hotel, and he and his father had climbed the Matterhorn.

It was dusk and Clive got up to switch on the lights. He had become so amiable that Neil was anticipating being asked to stay on, and trying to find a good reason for refusing. He did not fancy spending the night here. But Clive said:

"We'd better look you out a place to sleep. I'll lend a hand."

Relieved, Neil said: "That's all right. I'll find somewhere."

Clive insisted, though, on accompanying him. They found a bedroom in a large Victorian house behind the row of shops. A comfortable bed, Clive pointed out, bouncing on it, and with a bathroom next door.

"But you can come over to the caravan and shower in the morning," he added. "And breakfast with me. I've got some American bacon and I can make an omelette from powdered egg. Mushroom omelette – you like that?"

It was a relief to see him depart; Neil decided that in the morning he would definitely go his own way. He hung up his anorak, pausing to listen to a cry he recognized as that of a fox. There was no distinction between town and country now that men had gone. He was full from the meal, and tired. It did not take him long to drop off.

He awoke in the night with the impression of having heard a movement close by. He remembered he was no longer alone in the world, and called out: "Clive?" There was no answer, but his nerves remained taut. Mad, he had thought, but harmless – but could he be certain of that?

There was moonlight outside; sufficient for him to be sure there was no-one in the room. The door, though, was opened wider than it had been. A gust of wind, perhaps, but the night was still. He got out of bed, closed the door, and tugged a chest-of-drawers across to block it. As he did so he heard a sound again, outside and going away. An animal, he guessed.

He went back to bed and after a time slept soundly: it was bright day when he awoke again. He did not bother washing – the thought of the shower was tempting even if Clive's company was not – but threw on his clothes and left the house.

It was only about fifty yards to the main street, and he could see the Jaguar before he got there. The sleek shape hugged the road. It looked lower somehow. He came to the road junction and stared in disbelief. There was a reason for it looking lower: the tyres were flat.

Neil walked, frowning, towards the car. The tyres had been slashed savagely. He looked inside. The upholstery had been slashed as well, and the leather hung in strips.

It made no sense. Clive? It could scarcely be anyone else. He began to get angry. Mad or not, this was something to answer for. He found his fists clenching as he walked round the bend in the road to where the caravan was parked. The pedestrian crossing was there; but the two vehicles which had been immediately beyond it were gone.

The sounds in the night. . . . He was certain now that it had been Clive, but could not think why. Presumably he had been carrying a knife, since he had slashed the tyres and upholstery. Had he been planning to stick it into him, too? Neil shook his head, pushing his hands deep into his anorak pockets. He still could not envisage him as a murderer.

Gradually, as he brooded on it, he became aware of something – or aware, rather, of something missing. His right hand should be feeling the small round hardness of his mother's ring, but there was nothing there. It had been in the pocket when he hung up the anorak the night before. He had touched it before he went to bed, as he

70

always did.

Neil understood at last. It explained the determination to have him stay, and the solicitude in helping him find a place for the night. A place Clive knew, and into which he could creep while Neil slept. He must have been slipping out again when Neil called, but not before he had got what he came for.

But why? What did he want with an ordinary ring when he had a chest stuffed with jewels? But even as he framed the question, Neil realized how pointless it was. You might as well ask why a jackdaw stole.

He was still angry, but he pitied him as well. To be driven by that sick frantic greed, and to live in a world where, with almost infinite possibilities for indulging it, it could never be satisfied. It was miserable, really.

Neil turned and walked back slowly towards the Jaguar. He stared at the ripped seats. Not so miserable that he wouldn't cheerfully boot him, if he ever got the chance.

SEVEN

NEIL MOVED SEVERAL TIMES during his first week in London, before settling into a big house facing Hyde Park, not far from Wellington Barracks. He learned from papers in a desk that it had been the home of a foreign diplomat. It was very luxurious, with heavy brocade curtains and thick pile carpeting. The furnishings were to match, and he recognized some of the oil paintings on the walls as the work of famous artists.

The luxury was not his main reason for choosing it as a permanency. More important was the park in front, which meant he had a wide landscape rather than a narrow street to scan hopefully for an approaching figure; and the fact that the Serpentine was one of the nearer features of the landscape. Water ran from the taps still, but he felt happier with a broad expanse of fresh water within sight and reach.

Additionally the house was strategically placed, halfway between Knightsbridge and Kensington High Street, for access to shops; and shops that had served a markedly affluent population. The supplies were just about inexhaustible. And these considerations, he thought, were likely to attract other survivors, if they had not already done so.

His hopes for that varied. Immediately after the encounter with Clive he had felt optimistic. The world was empty no longer: there was a prospect of finding someone around every next corner. Even while he was searching for a replacement for the Jaguar he felt there was a chance of it happening. Now and then he stopped to halloo, and once half-fancied he heard a call in reply. He stopped and listened, and shouted and listened again, but only silence answered him.

Optimism remained as he continued the journey into London, in a blue Cortina. (There wasn't much in the tank, but he was in an almost continuously built-up area now, with abandoned cars on every side). Wherever the road offered anything of a vantage point, he stopped the car and scanned the horizon. Once he saw a plume of smoke rising in the distance, and set out to track it down. It involved a long detour, and he lost his way and had to re-locate the smoke from the upper room of a house, but he found it in the end. A whole row of houses had burned down, and the plume rose from a still smouldering section in the middle.

The sort of fire which had sent Rye up like a torch was unlikely here, of course. This was late twentieth, not seventeenth century London, its buildings more widely separated and built not of wood but brick and concrete and steel. Fires were self-limiting. In some places the area of devastation was quite large, but in general the city looked untouched.

And the stillness, the absence of movement, gave him a new understanding of the vastness of the place. As street succeeded empty street, Neil could not believe that he would not find someone soon. He stopped at Bromley to search more thoroughly and spent the night there. He made prolonged searches again in Clapham and Brixton. He drove for long periods with his thumb on the horn button, halting now and then with it still blaring to give anyone who heard it a chance to reach him.

Despondency, when it finally set in, was deeper than before. He reminded himself that nothing Clive had told him could be relied on. If the Earl of Blenheim had been a figment of imagination, might not the survivors he had spoken of be equally so? He knew one other person had lived through the Plague, but that did not mean two had. He and mad Clive might well be the total remaining population of Britain.

He came across indications, too, which suggested that, as far as the recent past was concerned, he had been quite wrong in his view of London as likely to attract people. It was not the fires, though they might well have driven people away; there were signs that the rat menace here had been appalling. Plenty were still about, by day as well as night, and at the height of their population expansion they must have become a brown tide of devastation. Everywhere heaps of bones lay bleaching in the streets. There were skeletons looking like those of cats or dogs, and once what had probably been a horse. Twice he found human skeletons; there was no way of telling whether they had succumbed to the Plague, or rats had pulled them down.

By the time he got to Princes Gate he had given up the idea of actively looking for others, and decided to stay put. He felt something like he had done as a child in Hampton Court maze, except that this maze was a million times more vast. He and the others, if there were any others, could be boxing and coxing in a hopelessly self-defeating fashion: the very morning he was away searching might be the morning someone came through here. He remembered a saying of his grandfather: that if you took up a position at Piccadilly Circus, sooner or later you would meet everyone you knew. He had thought it absurd, but saw the force of the argument now.

He did make one expedition, though. Increasingly, as

the days went by, his thoughts of Clive became less hostile. Mad or not, he was a human being. Even fantasies and kleptomania might be preferable to being alone. He thought of his remark about the Crown Jewels, and set off for the Tower of London.

The thing that amazed him was that the ravens were still there, strutting on the green beside the White Tower. But no Beefeaters, no milling crowds of tourists, no guides lecturing on the dramas of the past. These buildings which had known the tread of feet for over a thousand years did so no more. The only traces of humanity were the initials carved on the walls, and the rows of empty armour in the museum.

The heavy door leading to the Wakefield Tower was closed, and would not yield when he tried to open it. Locked, he supposed, before the end came – the last of the Beefeaters performing a final duty. It had been a fruitless errand. There was no way of knowing whether or not Clive had come here. And what difference would it have made, if he had? He would have taken his baubles and gone his way.

Neil went up on the battlements and looked across the river. Tower Bridge was lowered, and there was no tall ship demanding passage. The tide lapped aimlessly against the pillars. Further up in the Pool he could see the masts of ships, but as deserted and decaying as the silent roofs all round. He thought of the old days, and the constant busy traffic: barges, tugs, river boats, police launches. A few seagulls soared and swooped, with hoarse mewing cries. Not many, though. There was no never-failing supply of human refuse to support the vast army of scavengers of yore.

Gazing at the river, the focus of trade since before the Romans came, Neil had the shattering realization that what had happened had happened not just here but all over the world. He had been thinking of himself as lost and alone in the vastness of England; but it was not just one small island, it really was the whole planet. The thought was unbearable: he turned and quickly went away.

His life developed into a routine again. He rose about seven, washed and dressed and made breakfast. In the morning he walked in the Park when the weather was fine, and found himself automatically following the same route every day – past the Albert Memorial, along to the Round Pond, back to the bridge and across it to the Serpentine's north bank, over to Marble Arch for a glance, soon desultory, down deserted Oxford Street; then a return parallel with the mausoleum hotels of Park Lane, and along the tree-lined avenue of Rotten Row.

In the afternoon he visited the shops, or prepared fuel for his fire. The house was well supplied with central heating radiators, but the upstairs sitting room also had a hearth recessed under a white marble mantel, with an old-fashioned metal-basket fireplace. Neil had found saws and choppers, and he raided surrounding houses for wood. At first he did his best to take only valueless stuff – kitchen chairs and tables and such – but as he used up those within easy reach he grew less scrupulous. On a day which had dawned wet and during which rain soaked down without a break, he felt the house next door was as far as he wanted to venture. He staggered back with the remains of a pretty Pembroke table and several strips of panelling from the library.

He read a lot during bad weather. Some books he kept, against the possibility of wanting to read them again, but most went on the fuel pile. He found an old copy of *The Swiss Family Robinson*, which he started with fascination. The events were improbable and the characters fairly unbelievable, but he felt a morbid interest in the situation of people stranded on a desert island without resources. His own position was almost exactly the reverse. He had got used to not having electricity, radio and television, things like that. What remained was an incredible surplus: more food than he could ever eat and the whole of a metropolitan city for shelter. If he chose he could sleep in a different bed every night and die of old age – normal old age – with more than ninety nine per cent of them unused.

The Robinsons, on the other hand, had each other's company – voices, the sight of a smiling face, the touch of hands. He found the book too much for him in the end, and it went on the fire half-read.

The days were beginning to draw in, and the air at times had an autumnal touch. One day a gale blew up and raged for three days almost without let-up. Neil stayed indoors; fortunately he had laid in a good supply of fuel beforehand. He had food and books, and an ample supply of batteries for a splendid cassette player he had acquired. He told himself things could be a great deal worse.

It was good, all the same, to get out again into the fresh air. There was a brisk breeze still, gusting strongly, but only a few clouds chased across the blue sky. He felt exhilarated, and took deep breaths as he walked along the gravel path through what had once been the carefully tended gardens at the foot of the Memorial. Weeds grew thickly in them, and were pushing through the path as well. Further off what had been lawn was long lush grass, almost knee high.

A few flowers survived to provide splashes of brighter colour, but the prevailing hue was green. Because of this the unexpected patch of red stood out. It was snarled in a tall briar – a standard rose that had already reverted to the primitive – and his first thought was that it was a late-flowering rose blossom. On closer view he saw it was a child's balloon. It was sagging, more than half deflated, and he was continuing on his walk, uninterested, when he saw it had something white attached to it, a small square of card. There was writing on it.

The briar was tall and protected by other tangled growth. Neil had to force his way in, and pull the briar down to get at the balloon. The small piece of pasteboard was limp, its edges soggy from rain, but Scotch tape had been stuck across the part carrying the message. The message itself was short and very simple:

I am at 34 Heath Avenue,
Hampstead. Where are you?

Passing through Piccadilly Circus, Neil thought again of his grandfather's remark. Anyone who waited here now in the hope of seeing a friend would be likely to have a long vigil. But one did not look for friends any more – any human being was a friend. There had been no name on the card and it had crossed his mind that it might have come from Clive. That did not bother him, either. All that mattered was that it was someone alive, and seeking contact.

He had looked up Heath Avenue in a London street guide, and had mapped out the best route before he set off. Despite that he lost his way a couple of times. Once the road was blocked by debris, where fire had caused a large building to collapse outwards. Backtracking, he found himself confronted by a No Entry sign. He thought, driving past it, of the innumerable rules and regulations men had had to devise to enable them to live together on an overcrowded planet. There was only one rule left: find someone.

He wondered about the sender of the message. He doubted if it could have been Clive. It was not the sort of thing Clive would do, and the actual message seemed too simple and straightforward to have come from him. The writing had been neat and attractive, well-formed without being ornate. Someone about his own age, he guessed.

The sense of anticipation was beyond anything he could remember. It was like waiting for Christmas when he was little, but no Christmas Eve had ever been like this. It occurred to him, starting up the long slope of Haverstock Hill, that he did not know what sex the stranger was: the writing could have been either. That was unimportant, too. Soon, very soon, there would be a meeting, an end to

78

being alone.

He made a conscious effort to cut down the mounting excitement he felt, deliberately seeking difficulties and objections. He had no idea, for instance, how long the balloon and its card had been blowing about London – for weeks or months possibly. Whoever had sent it might have grown tired of waiting for a reply and moved on. This could be a wild goose chase.

But his mood of expectancy and optimism easily withstood that particular cavil. The message itself was real, beyond doubt. Even if the person sending it had moved, there would be another message saying where. Having made that attempt at communication, he was scarcely likely to leave a blank trail for someone responding to it.

It was more likely, Neil thought with increasing animation, that he might find not one survivor but several. Probably quite a number of balloons had been launched, hundreds maybe, and others discovered sooner. There might be a whole group of people in Heath Avenue when he got there.

He found open country surrounding him and realized he had missed his way again and gone through Hampstead to the Heath. It was annoying but at least he knew he was very close to his objective. He swung the car round in an arc that ran it over the pavement, barely missing a fence, and drove back. He wondered if they might have heard the noise of the engine, and come out to look for him.

Heath Avenue was a broad road, flanked by trees whose branches bore yellowing leaves that floated down in the path of the car, and by tall red brick houses. No-one had turned out, but the slight feeling of let-down went as he caught sight of No 34. He had no need to check the number: a sheet spread across the front, each end secured to a window, carried in bold black paint the single word:

WELCOME.

A sports car was standing outside, its relatively clean windscreen evidence of recent use. Neil parked behind it, and got out. He ought to have put up a sign outside his own house, he realized. For that matter, he should have thought of something like the balloons. The inhabitant of No 34 was obviously more enterprising.

The front door was latched but not locked. He opened it and stepped into the hall. He called out:

"Hi, there! Anyone home?"

There was no reply. He had a moment's disappointment, but only that. At this time of day, he himself would have been more likely to be out than in. The stranger would have his own routine of walks and foraging.

A residue of old habits and etiquette suggested that he ought not to make himself free of someone else's house without the owner's invitation: he should wait on the step or outside in the car. But he realized how silly that was. The old ways were gone; ownership no longer had a meaning.

All the same, his exploration was tentative. The hall, he observed, was quite tidy, and he ventured further to find a kitchen with pots neatly stacked and working surfaces much cleaner than those he had left in Princes Gate. Cupboards were well stocked with food, and a Calor gas stove had been imported into an otherwise all-electric set-up. Crates of beer stood in a pile against one wall. The whole scene had an organized look.

He went upstairs, noting that the carpet on stairs and landing had been recently swept. An open door led to a large sitting room, equally clean and with the stamp of daily use. On a desk were two piles of heavy white cartridge paper, one blank, the other consisting of pencilled sketches. They must have been done by the person living here, because they were post-Plague. That showed not only in the emptiness of the streets he had drawn, but in particular things – a shattered shop window with goods in disarray, a skeleton at a road junction. The sketches were neat and realistic, the work of a draughtsman. Near the window, though, stood an easel, with a half-finished oil painting. *That* was a frenzy of colours and shapes; Neil could not tell what it was meant to represent.

There was a bowl with apples, something Neil had not seen for a long time. There must be an orchard nearby. The bowl stood on a table, which also held a ledger-type book. He opened it to see writing – the handwriting that had been on the card – and to recognize it as a diary. He closed it, and went on looking round the room. On the mantel an atmospheric clock spun its circular brass weight to and fro, half a minute to each spin. Someone who wanted to keep track of time, an interest he had long abandoned.

He continued with his exploration. There was a bathroom across the way, again very clean, with a kettle in which hot water had presumably been carried up from the kitchen. The best solution, he decided, would be for both of them to abandon their present dens – to join in finding a place where a full hot water system, perhaps central heating as well, could be run off Calor gas. He was pleased with himself for the thought: he could be enterprising as well.

The door of the next room was ajar. Neil pushed it open and saw that the curtains were drawn and it was in shadow. He saw a bed made up, the whiteness of sheets . . . then the darker vertical shadow that hung in the centre of the room. The rope was secured to an old-fashioned brass light fitting; a chair was overturned on the carpet.

He just managed to reach the bathroom before being sick.

EIGHT

AFTERWARDS Neil retained no recollection of the drive back to Princes Gate, and only a blurred impression of the evening that followed. He remembered lethargy and chill and a headache. He went early to bed, wondering if he were getting a cold.

In the morning, though his thoughts were clearer, the headache and the weariness – a leaden feeling dragging down mind and body – were still present. He had not bothered to stock up with medicines – he had been in good health so far and there was a chemist's shop within easy reach. His father had been a great believer in massive doses of Vitamin C for aborting head-colds. He had just about made up his mind to get up and go out to get some when the thought struck him: whatever was wrong was not the common cold, or any other disease harboured by man. The whole brave company – not just the cold, but measles, chicken pox, poliomyelitis, glandular fever and the rest – had found oblivion along with the creature who for millenia had been their host and victim.

He stayed in bed all that day and most of the next. It had not been an illness at all, he realized later, but shock: arising not only from the sight of the hanging body, the head slumped to one side, but from the shattering of hopes. Along with that went a bitter awareness of the narrowness of the margin by which the hopes had failed. Hours – certainly no more than twenty four. A watch had been ticking on the dangling wrist when he touched the cold flesh. If he had found the balloon a day sooner – if he had set out sooner from Princes Gate. . . .

Despair and self-recrimination ran their course and were superseded by another emotion: curiosity. In his mind there was the image of death, a horror that could still shock for all that he had seen since the Plague came. He had a desperate need for something more than that. This had been a boy like himself, who had survived as he had, and tried to go on living in the deserted world. He felt he must know more about him, be able to think of him as something other than a dangling corpse.

The notion of going back there was unthinkable, but in the moment of revulsion at the thought he remembered something. Before he fled the house he had picked up the diary. It must still be in the pocket of his anorak.

Neil read it that evening, by candlelight.

The style of writing was clear, simple and neat like the sketches, and the thoughts expressed had a similar clarity. He had been in the middle of reading Daniel Defoe's "Journal of the Plague Years" when the new Plague struck; and that had decided him to keep a journal.

He had been at a boarding school in the west country which had been one of the earliest to close down and send its pupils home. And home, Neil realized with surprise, had been the place where he had found him. His father had been something to do with shipping, and apart from his parents he had an elder brother at University and a sister who was a photographic model.

It appeared to have been a warm, close family. When disaster struck, they stayed together. They too had rejected the mass burials. His mother had died first, and

83

they had buried her in the garden. The others had gone in their turn: he had buried his brother last. It was set down calmly, with no show of emotion.

Yet the sense of gradual but inexorable destruction was chilling. Neil compared it with his own case – the sharp numbing impact of total disaster. He saw how much less bearable the other might be; and for the first time realized how what had happened that rainy Saturday afternoon had been a shield against subsequent events. He had thought he understood the horror of it all, but it had not really been so. Certain things had made an impact – his grandparents' death and the death of Tommy and Susie in particular – but even there the pain had been blunted for him. They had been reefs looming out of a mist, with the mist rapidly closing again to obliterate them.

For Peter Cranbell on the other hand – the name was written inside the cover of the journal – there had been a steady progression into grief and misery. A page was left blank after the entry that recorded his brother's death. The next entry stood on a page by itself:

"I want to die, but can't."

After that the recording of events was resumed, carefully written and dated. He had fled from the stench of death to live in a tent on the Heath; but returned before the rat explosion. He had barricaded himself in for a couple of weeks when that was at its height and wrote of watching them from his window, listening to their high-pitched squeaking – eventually witnessing the carnage when they turned on one another. He had stayed inside for some time after, only venturing out again when a shortage of food forced him to do so.

Peter Cranbell, obviously, had put a lot of thought and effort into coping with the situation following the Plague. He had been more practical and methodical than Neil; more imaginative, too. That was illustrated by his scheme for sending the balloons out. He had picked a windy day, the wind from the north-west quarter, and launched them from the top floor of the house, watching them bob away and vanish over the massed roofs of London.

The entry was dated August 29th. Neil would not have known how long ago that had been – he himself had made no attempt to keep track of dates – but for the remainder of the journal. Day followed day with brief but precise accounts of his activities. Having written of the launching of the balloons, there was no further reference to them; until the last item but one. It read:

"Two months exactly since I sent off the balloons. There is no point in thinking anyone will come now. I suppose I could try again with another batch, but I can't summon up the enthusiasm."

In the final entry he referred, for the first time, to his sketching:

"I remember the answer some writer gave to the question: would a true writer still go on writing, marooned on a desert island? He said probably yes, but only provided he had a guarantee the ink wouldn't fade and the hope, however slim, that some day a ship would come, bringing people who could read.

"He meant you can do without an audience but not without the hope of an audience, some time, somehow. I took my sketch pad with me as usual when I went for a walk this morning, but brought it back unopened. There's no point in going on drawing things.

"There's no point in going on."

Neil closed the book, and sat looking at it. Peter Cranbell had organized his new life efficiently – much more efficiently than Neil had done. The candle flames flickered in a draught from a crack in the window he had been meaning to see to for more than a week. Peter Cranbell would have fixed it. Peter Cranbell, for that matter, had not made do with candles: he had found lamps, and oil to burn in them.

Then, with the same calm efficiency, he had decided the life he had organized was not worth continuing; and had practically set about organizing his death.

Neil looked up with a shudder at the light fitting above his head. The rope carefully noosed round the neck, the chair kicked away . . . he could never nerve himself for that. But there were other, easier methods. A chemist's shop – finding the pills and swallowing them, and just going to sleep. He felt very tired and the idea of sleep was attractive – sleep going on and on, with no new days of loneliness to face. He stumbled towards his bed, pulling off his clothes and dropping them as he went.

He slept heavily and woke in the morning with a sense of depression that at first had no particular focus. It was a moment or two before he remembered Peter Cranbell, and the resolve he had reached, or thought he reached. In the grey light he saw his clothes scattered on the floor, where he had let them fall. Peter Cranbell, he thought, would have hung them up tidily, however tired he was.

Neil stretched his arms, yawning. The feeling of gloom lifted. His life was much less orderly than the other's had been, but perhaps for that reason he had not come to the end of its resources – to the final loss of hope. The chemist's shop, at any rate, had lost its attraction.

He went out to wash, and found himself whistling. He stopped, thinking of Peter Cranbell; then shrugged and continued.

Neil settled back into his usual habits as the days passed. He had vague intentions of doing something constructive, such as sending out message-balloons of his own or fixing a banner in front of the house or at some salient point nearby. He thought, too, of keeping a beacon fire going in the street, or out in the park.

In the end he did nothing. He told himself it was because they were all futile exercises – neither balloons nor banner had worked for Peter Cranbell, and as far as a beacon was concerned it would not be likely to attract attention, anyway. There was usually smoke rising somewhere on the horizon from some self-engendered fire.

But the real reason, as he finally admitted, was that to do anything would be to set hope in motion again, and he could not bear the thought of disillusionment. It was not that he believed any longer that he was a sole survivor. If three had come through, why not thirty – or three hundred? But of the two he had found, one had been mad and the second dead. He had a strange feeling, a kind of fear of what might come of a third encounter.

When he first settled in Princes Gate he had several times gone foraging in Harrods. Subsequently he had started going the other way, towards Kensington High Street, and as with other aspects of his life the tendency had fixed into a routine. He had not been near the huge department store for over a month when he decided, one brisk chilly morning, to revisit it.

He had the Food department as his main objective, but did not go there right away. He went up the motionless escalator to the first floor, beaming a torch ahead of him, and headed south through Furnishings. Some of the furniture looked attractive: a leather sofa, in particular, would have made a useful addition to his sitting room. But he could not have lifted it single-handed, let alone transported it. A small armchair he did lift, and decided he could have carried it with some effort. He put it down again: not worth the trouble.

He went through to Books, his torch picking out rows of volumes gathering dust. He propped the torch on a table and picked out one or two books at random. *Politics for the Ordinary Citizen; Every Man His Own Lawyer.* . . . Neil let them drop on the floor. *The Can-Opener Cook* was more to

87

the point: he put that in his haversack.

And then shelf after shelf of novels – people's imaginings about other people, processed through elaborate systems of production for yet other people to read. A section was headed Science-Fiction: hundreds and hundreds of exciting futures for the human race. All boiled down to one. Or rather, none. But he supposed if one looked at it from a more detached viewpoint there were compensations. All those forests, for instance, which no longer needed to be destroyed to make paper.

In the Pet Shop he saw displays of food, dog chews and catnips, baskets and rubber balls and vitamins, brushes and combs and shampoos, leads and chains and training whistles. The dogs, swept out by the rats, were beginning to come back: a pack of a dozen or so had run snarling past his house the previous day. They looked wilder than the ones he had seen immediately following the Plague. He doubted if a training whistle would have much effect on them.

He entered a vast room in which the swinging beam flashed from screen to blank screen. Television sets. And elaborate and massive sound reproduction systems ranged along the sides. Neil went through to the pianos, solider and more friendly shapes, a score or more stretching away into the darkness. He remembered winter evenings, and the sound of Amanda's practising floating up through the house while he did his prep. He found one open, and strummed the keys idly: the notes soared and died. He had started to learn, too, when he was younger, but he had been bored and his parents had not insisted on his continuing. He regretted that now. It would have been nice to be able to make music.

He went downstairs and at last to the Food Hall. The smell of the rotted perishables was very faint, barely perceptible. He had kept on the whole to a fairly narrow range of diet, ringing the changes on things he liked, but today he felt adventurous and looked for more exotic

88

items. Quails' eggs in aspic, pressed boar's head, haggis, venison steaks, occra, salsify, sauerkraut. . . . He picked up tins of kangaroo meat and rattlesnake, but put those back on the shelf. Cherries in brandy, on the other hand, struck him as worth taking.

Tins of curry powder. . . . His grandfather had been fond of curries and that – curried lamb usually – had been their regular Tuesday supper. He hefted the tin, trying to remember the details of his grandmother's preparations. He had a hazy recollection of sliced onions simmering golden-yellow in butter, and the curry powder being added to brown with them. How much, though? A teaspoonful? Or a table spoon? And hadn't there been flour, as well? He had no butter, but plenty of margarine in sealed packs. He decided to have a go, and added the tin of curry powder to the rest.

That was enough for today, he decided. He made his way back but by an unfamiliar route. He found himself traversing Cosmetics, his beam lighting up names which had presumably once been significant: Coty, Elizabeth Arden, Rochas, Dior, Rubinstein. And little counters, piled high with jars and bottles and cases of lipsticks. The display on one of the counters had collapsed, and the contents were spilled across the aisle. Neil was making a detour of the mess when something on the fringe of the torch beam caught his eye. He stopped, and looked more closely. A bottle had broken, producing a pool of some white substance. But the whiteness was not complete. It was marred by something – the clear imprint of a shoe.

Neil told himself it meant nothing. It could have happened months ago. At the height of the Plague, perhaps – with some woman searching the empty store for something to cure the wrinkling of her skin, pulling down the display, maybe, in her despair and anger. But examining it more closely he noticed something else. This – he put out a tentative finger – was tacky. If the substance had been spilled long, it would have dried out. And the surface was snowy white; it had not yet collected the dust which lay thickly everywhere else.

He straightened up. Someone *had* been here, and recently. A girl: it was the mark of a girl's shoe, several sizes smaller than his own. He felt his heart pounding and suddenly, involuntarily, heard himself crying out:

"Hello! Hello?"

He felt foolish, listening to the echoes, but called again and again, for several minutes.

Afterwards he was more rational, and planned things. He had always used the doors at the north-west corner, but there might be other ways in and out. He checked carefully, and found that the main door, in Brompton Road, had also been forced, but that the rest were locked. He returned to the Stationery department, found two white cards and a black fibre-tip marker, and wrote his message on each:

"My name is Neil Miller. I am at 170 Princes Gate."

He thought for a moment, then added:

"Opposite Hyde Park."

He placed a card in each entrance, conspicuously so that no-one coming in could avoid seeing it. For an hour or two afterwards he still hung about the store; it was improbable that she would come back again so soon, but he was reluctant to go away. Eventually hunger made him go.

Neil thought about it as he prepared his meal. His general feeling had been that if he did find someone else it would be of his own sex. That probably stemmed from an ingrained belief that the female was the weaker – that with odds against survival so high, only males could be expected to have come through.

But there was no rational ground for thinking it. There had been nothing to suggest that women were more susceptible to the Plague than men – the only forbearance it had shown, and that minimal, had been towards the young rather than the old. And subsequent conditions of life, though strange, had not been particularly hard or dangerous, requiring special strength. After the rat menace had flared and died, all that was needed was a reasonable ability to take care of oneself. A girl might even be better equipped from that point of view.

Plus, he thought, remembering Peter Cranbell, the ability to sustain loneliness. He felt the crushing weight of that more than he had done for some time: the thought of another living person, within reach perhaps, sharpened the awareness of being on his own, not just in this room in this house, but with thousands of empty houses surrounding him.

He wondered what she would be like. The small footprint made him picture a slim girl, quick in her movements. With fair hair, long but very neat – braided, perhaps. Not blue eyes, though: brown. And a quiet voice, with a lilt to it.

Neil found himself smiling. Creating a girl, down to hair and eyes and voice, on the basis of a solitary footprint: how ridiculous! But ridiculous or not, the image was not easily dismissed. He thought of her as he went to sleep and saw her clearly. She was wearing a light blue dress, with white cuffs and collar.

For the next two days he went to Harrods both morning and afternoon. The cards were where he had left them but he still called out, with no response. On his second visit on the third day, though, the card he had left in the main entrance was gone.

Neil stared at the place where it had been. The previous day he had gone again to the Cosmetics department, to reassure himself of the footprint's reality, but even so the episode had begun to seem unreal. He found it hard to believe in the stranger's existence. If she did exist, the visit had been a chance one, not to be repeated. But she had come back! As the fact penetrated, he found himself shouting again:

"Hello! Where are you? Hello . . . hello. . . !"

He stopped abruptly. Having discovered the card, obviously she had gone to Princes Gate, to look for him. He made for home, running most of the way. He called to her outside the house and went inside, racing through the rooms. There was no-one there, and no message. He could have outpaced her, he told himself, and stared out of the window. Birds fluttered through the air and he saw a scuttling rat: nothing else.

He waited for an hour. He had another idea – that she might have come, found no-one at home, and gone back to the store. She might have left a message in replacement of his. He retraced his steps but found nothing – called out again, but knew it to be futile.

That night he gave it a lot of thought. She had taken his message, but not responded. There could be a reason: frightening things might have happened to her. But he would not accept a refusal of contact. Whether or not she wanted it, there must be a meeting.

Neil reviewed the shreds of information he had. Since she had come to the store a second time it was unlikely that she was a transient. He had heard no engine sound – and *would* have done this time because he had been on the alert – which meant she had travelled on foot. Almost certainly, in that case, she was living within a couple of miles' radius of Harrods. He was confident he would find her.

He started the search early next morning, and spent the day driving around. All he achieved was a fuller awareness of what a warren London was; and the unhappy realization that in guessing her mode of transport he had overlooked a third possibility. It could have been a bicycle, which made the potential range much greater.

It was with this in mind that he had what he thought was a brainwave. He remembered the dinging bells of burglar alarms, harshly calling attention to themselves. They had depended on electrical power, but there was something that didn't, and would be heard over a far greater area.

The first church he found was itself equipped with an electrical bell system, but the second had ropes. He heaved on one, and heard the bell clang out high above. He rang and rang, pulling until his arms were sore; then found a pew and sat down. Sparrows had found a way in before him and chattered up in the rafters. Hugging his aching shoulders he realized what a fool he had been – how absurd the brainwave. If she had not come in response to the card, why should she answer a peal of bells?

Something else was also clear: the car had been a mistake. She would have heard him, streets away. If he was going to track her down, he must use stealth.

Neil thought of the acres of interlocking streets, the vast area within easy cycling distance of the store. There must be a way of limiting the range. The thing to remember was that she had been facing the same problems as himself, and had very likely come to similar solutions. He had chosen Princes Gate for comfort, and for access to a good supply of fresh water. Was there an alternative location, offering the same possibilities?

He did not have to think long: the answer was obvious. The best water supply possible – better than the Serpentine – was the Thames. And riverside Chelsea abounded in comfortable houses. That was where he should concentrate his search.

Neil took rations for several days, and spare batteries for his torch. He picked out his sturdiest pair of shoes, but on reflection abandoned them in favour of some with crepe soles. It was not too cold – grey but mild – but he crammed a jersey in. He wanted to be prepared for a long expedition.

He passed through the museums area of South Kensington on his way, and remembered Saturday afternoons, and ice-creams sold from barrows. The gutters were choked and the forecourt of the tube station, where the paper-boys had shouted, was thick with accumulated dirt and rubbish. He trudged on south, to Sloane Square and the King's Road. Behind the grimy glass window of a boutique, models struck weird gymnastic poses, and a sign said: THIS YEAR THIS IS IT!

The big private houses near the river were the best bet, and he headed that way. But there were so many of them, so many once-affluent tree-lined streets. He studied the houses he passed for signs of occupancy. If she were avoiding people she would probably try not to leave any, but something might give her away. He thought he was on to something when he saw a trail worn across what had been a small lawn, but it led him to a large hole under a wall – a fox's earth, most likely.

He took a break for a snack, and pushed on grimly. He kept at it until after dusk had fallen before finding a place to spend the night. He stayed in the big ground-floor sitting room where there was a comfortable settee. It was old-fashioned, well supplied with family photographs in silver frames. They did not interest him any longer.

Three more days of fruitless tramping followed. He was discouraged, and wondered if he could have guessed wrong about the district. She might not have had his idea about a fresh water supply, or she might have picked a different stretch of the river bank. The south side, perhaps, even though the houses were smaller and less luxurious there.

His luck changed unexpectedly. He had finished the provisions in his haversack; he thought of going back home, but decided it would be easier to forage near at

94

hand. He went to the nearest supermarket in the King's Road, and smashed a way in. There was plenty of food, but also sections of shelf which had been stripped. He looked more closely and saw the signs of a recent human presence: dust disturbed on the shelves and floor.

Neil followed the track. It led not to the door he had broken, but out to the back. There was a yard, and a steel gate. The gate was padlocked, but the chain had been severed with metal cutters.

From that point all he had to do was wait. He found an upper room across the street with a view of the gate, drew a chair up to the window, and settled down. He watched carefully all that day, and most of the next.

Even so, he missed her; she had probably entered the store while he was in the bathroom. He looked out to see the gate opening, and at the same time realized he had not noticed an addition to the scene – an old-fashioned lady's bicycle, with a basket in front of the handlebars, leaning against the wall further down.

Neil ran for the stairs. She was getting on the bicycle as he came out of the front door. He did not call, but raced towards her.

She heard him; and without looking round started to pedal away. If she had had another second or two she would have outdistanced him, but he managed to get close enough to grab the carrier at the back. The metal cut into his fingers and a backward-kicking foot bruised his arm, but he held on. The bicycle swerved, and she fell.

NINE

KEEPING HIS VOICE as casual as possible, Neil said:

"I'm sorry, but. . . . Are you all right?"

There was no reply from the figure on the ground. He did not think she was injured, but the fall might have winded her. He stooped and took an arm.

"Let me help you."

She rejected his hand, but got up on her own. He could not see her properly until she was standing. Thick fair hair was pulled back under a cap from a pointed face. The figure, shapeless in a short padded coat and trousers, matched his own in height. He felt a shock of disappointment: it was not a girl, but a boy.

He repeated: "Are you all right?" The face stared sullenly. "Sorry if I took you by surprise."

They looked at one another. There was a response at last, a brief shrug.

"I'm all right."

The voice, low-pitched in a vaguely northern accent, was feminine. He could see now that it was a girl's figure as well. But a bit of a far cry from the one he had imagined.

At least, though, it was a fellow human being. He

smiled, in an attempt at reassurance. She was wary and timid, possibly with good reason. Any approach would have alarmed her, let alone a full-blooded chase and tackle.

He asked: "Where are you living?"

She hesitated slightly. "In Chelsea."

Tins and packages had been spilt from the basket. Neil gathered them and righted the bicycle, while she watched. Holding the handlebars, he said:

"I'm Neil Miller. What's your name?"

She looked at him doubtfully. "Docket. Billie Docket."

"I'll walk you back, Billie."

Her figure tensed. "No."

"Look," he said, "I'm not going to hurt you. Not in any way. I realize things may have been rough. They could be rougher still in time to come. It makes sense to help one another."

She shook her head. "I'm all right."

The note of dismissal was unmistakeable, but Neil would not accept it. He smiled at her; unnaturally, he felt, but he kept it fixed. He said flatly:

"I'm coming with you."

She was unresponsive still, but seemed to recognize an inevitability. She nodded and set out walking, with Neil pushing the bicycle at her side.

His efforts to make conversation, though, were not very successful. To direct questions she gave terse unforthcoming replies. No, she had not been in London all the time. Where had she come from? Derby. When had she come to London? A while back. Had she met other survivors? A look, another shrug. No.

He had a feeling she might not be telling the truth there, but whatever she was concealing was plainly something she did not want to talk about. Something unpleasant, probably: it would not be a good idea to press the point. He stopped questioning, and talked about his own experiences. She stayed silent, apparently uninterested. It did

97

not look as though she were likely to provide either stimulating or restful companionship. But she was alive. He told her about the balloon, and finding Peter Cranbell's body. She made no comment. Then abruptly she said:

"I want to go in here."

The sign said LADIES. Neil watched her go in. He propped the bicycle against the wall and gazed along the street. In the dusk of a grey afternoon it looked almost normal. Next year, though, with the spring growth, there would be a difference. How long before the saplings reached roof level?

It was very quiet, of course, a stillness to which he had become accustomed. The click was faint, but it alerted him. He ran round to the back of the convenience: a small window was open and she was half out of it. They stared at each other in silence; then she dropped down inside and came out by the way she had entered.

Neil said: "I'm really not going to attack you, or anything. You do believe that, don't you?"

She did not answer, and he did not pursue it. They walked side by side without talking. He was trying to puzzle her out. She was obviously scared of him, yet somehow did not give that impression. But whatever it was, he knew he must be patient.

They were in Chelsea, walking through the streets he had fruitlessly searched. This was one like all the rest, Something-Gardens. He thought he detected a difference in her, an added tension. She slowed slightly, then walked faster. He suspected she might be on the point of making another break for it, and prepared to ditch the bicycle. Instead she stopped dead, as a voice broke the stillness:

"Billie!"

It came from a house they had just passed. Neil saw another girl, leaning out of an upper window and waving. He turned to Billie.

"I thought you said you hadn't met anyone else?"

98

She did not reply, but turned and walked back to the house. Neil followed with the bicycle. It was not surprising he had passed the place before without noticing anything. There was no indication of anyone living here; and fallen leaves had been carefully strewn over path and steps. It provided an effective camouflage.

Billie pushed open the door. Neil followed close as she went in, in case she attempted to slam and bolt it on him; but her attention was all on the slim figure running downstairs.

"I couldn't understand why you were going past." She halted a step or two from the bottom, and looked over Billie's shoulder towards Neil. "Who is it?"

The hall was lit only by a fanlighting over the door, and it was not possible to make out her apprearance very clearly. She was smaller than Billie, a little younger probably, and Neil knew at once it had been her footprint he had seen. Her voice was lighter, more animated than the other's. It had a soft country burr.

Billie did not immediately answer the question, so he did it for her.

"I'm Neil Miller. I found her outside the Supermarket."

She was studying him carefully, but he did not get the same impression of antagonism he had had with Billie. She asked:

"Was it you rang the bells?"

"Yes."

There was a pause. Her look was considering still. He said:

"I'm not dangerous, I promise."

"You don't sound dangerous." She paused again. "I'm Lucy Stephens. You'd better come up, rather than just stand there."

He followed them both to the first floor. Lucy led the way into a sitting room, the one from whose window she had waved. It was lighter than downstairs, but shadowy

99

from the growing dusk outside. Lucy pulled curtains across: they were of a heavy material, and he observed that she tweaked them fully into place so that not a chink of light showed through. They were in pitch blackness until she switched on a lantern-torch, and put on others in different parts of the room. They were rigged up with pretty shades.

When she had finished, she asked:

"Cup of tea?"

Neil nodded. "Thanks."

There was a primus stove in the hearth, and she bent down to pump and light it. Neil had a strange feeling as he watched her. It was a sort of calm excitement, a curiosity so deep that it seemed to twitch at his nerve ends; along with a weird sense of fear and boldness mixed up together.

He could see her more clearly in the light from the lantern-torches. She had a thin face, he thought at first, but corrected it: above a slight hollowness of cheek, the actual cheekbones were quite broad. Her forehead was high, nose small and slightly snub. In concentrating on the primus stove she bit her lower lip: her teeth were small and even, very white.

Apart from her slimness she bore no resemblance to the girl he had visualized. Her eyes were neither blue nor brown, but hazel. And she was brunette, her hair a very dark brown, almost black, curling at the ends.

She asked Billie: "Did you remember teabags?"

"Yes."

"Is the stuff still in the bike basket? Be a dear and bring it up."

Billie hesitated, but reluctantly went. Lucy looked up, brushing hair back from her face.

"You rang the bells in the hope of someone coming?" Neil nodded. "And no-one did?"

"No."

"We talked about it."

She sat back on her haunches. She wore a white skirt

100

and blouse, very fresh-looking. He said:

"And decided not to do anything?" She nodded. "Why?"

"Billie thought it was too risky. I suggested we might go along quietly to see, without showing ourselves, but she said it might be a trap." He looked at her in query. "There might have been more than one – others waiting in ambush."

"The blackout of the windows." He gestured towards the curtains. "And spreading leaves in front of the door – did Billie think of them?"

"Yes."

Billie came hurrying upstairs, her arms full. Neil said:

"And not replying to the message I left?"

Lucy wrinkled her brow. "Message?"

"In Harrods. After I found your footprint there."

"We have been in Harrods. A footprint?" She laughed. "Like Robinson Crusoe?"

"I put my name and address on cards, and left them in both doorways."

"We didn't see any cards."

"But one was taken."

Billie, who had been listening in silence, said:

"Blown away, maybe."

"I don't think so. It was quite heavy. And out of the wind."

"Or a rat took it. I've seen them carrying quite big things."

Neil did not comment on the improbability. He guessed she was lying again: she had found the card, and removed it before Lucy could spot it. But it would do no good to suggest that. The kettle was beginning to boil and Lucy bent towards it. He said only:

"I could do with a cup of tea."

Afterwards they talked. Neither girl had originally lived in London; like Neil they had been drawn to it by the promise of plenty. Lucy came from a village in Oxfordshire; her father had worked on the land. Her mother had died following the birth of a brother, when she was five. She had looked after the household from an early age. She referred to her father indifferently, and Neil gathered he had been a cold man, but he thought there were tears in her eyes when she spoke of her little brother.

She had met Billie while wandering through the outskirts of London. For her that had been the only contact since the Plague. Billie, on the other hand, had had encounters, she said: unpleasant ones. Neil asked in what way unpleasant?

He looked at Billie as he put the question, but she stared back mutely. Lucy said:

"She doesn't like talking about them. So don't ask."

She had told *him* that she had not met anyone. That had been to conceal the fact of Lucy's existence, but he wondered if anything she said was to be relied on. The unpleasant encounters could have been another lie, aimed at Lucy. Not pursuing that, either, he told again the story of Peter Cranbell. It troubled Lucy.

"How dreadful. . . . And if you'd managed to get there just a bit sooner. . . ."

"Yes."

Billie made a comment at last.

"He must have been weak-minded, to do something like that."

Neil looked at her. "How long did you have of it?"

"Of what?"

"Being on your own." He turned to Lucy. "Have you been together long?"

"A couple of months. Three, nearly."

"You don't get used to it. It gets worse, not better."

Lucy said: "I suppose it would. I hadn't thought. You didn't meet anyone, before us?"

"Only once. And only for a few hours."

He told them about Clive. Billie showed more interest.

102

She said:

"You can't say *he* wasn't mad."

She spoke with some satisfaction. Neil said: "Perhaps. Fairly harmless, though."

"Was he? He ripped your car up, didn't he? You were lucky he didn't use the knife on you." She spoke to Lucy, her whole stance excluding Neil. "It's like I've said. It doesn't make sense to take chances – to trust anyone, the way things are now. There's no policeman on the corner, and you can't dial 999."

"But you've got to take chances," Neil said. "How many people are there alive, do you think, in the whole of England? A few hundred? Less, probably. Some of them may be mad, some may be dangerous, but you can't just isolate yourself."

Billie regarded him with open hostility.

"Can't you?" She added, with emphasis: "We've been all right, on our own."

There was a silence, which Lucy ended.

"Anyway, you've found us. And you don't strike me as either mad or dangerous. The least we can do is ask you to stay to supper."

The hostile look was still fixed on Neil. He ignored it, and said to Lucy:

"That's kind of you. It'll be a pleasant change to sample someone else's cooking."

Rather to Neil's surprise, Billie cooked the meal. She was a good cook, using seasonings and spices to improve the flavour of the inevitable tinned meat and vegetables. She made him realize how primitive and inadequate his own techniques had been.

After supper she was mostly silent, while Neil and Lucy did the talking, but he found her silent presence oppressive. He tried to disregard it, and talked of the problems of the winter, now almost on them. For heating the girls had paraffin stoves, and a plentiful supply of fuel. (They had decided against open fires, he realized, because of the impossibility of disguising a smoking chimney: Billie's decision). Neil mentioned the Calor gas he had found in Peter Cranbell's house, and his idea of fitting gas cylinders into a central heating system.

Lucy was dubious. It would need skilled plumbing, she pointed out, and proper tools.

"I could find the tools," Neil said. "And a do-it-yourself plumbing manual I could learn from."

"Do you know where there's a supply of Calor gas cylinders?"

"No. But Peter Cranbell managed to find some. Clive, too. It shouldn't present that much of a problem."

"I think it's simpler carrying on as we are," Lucy said. "We've a heater in the bathroom for water. You can't have a proper bath, but it's better than nothing."

She spoke firmly, and once again Neil decided to let it go. He said:

"You're probably right. But it's something to keep in mind, for a permanent place."

"Permanent?"

"Well, we'll need to think about that, won't we? Somewhere in the county."

Billie broke her silence. "You push off to the country if you want. We're all right here."

"We all headed towards London for the same reason," Neil said. "We knew the supply position would be better – food, clothes and the rest. But it's no good in the long term."

Billie said: "I don't see why."

"Well, for a start we need fresh food. We're going short of vitamins. Eventually our health is bound to be affected."

"Plenty of vitamins in the chemist shops. More than enough."

"It's not the same as getting them naturally. We could keep chickens – have fresh eggs."

Lucy said: "Fresh eggs!"

It was a line to pursue, Neil thought. "And milk."

Lucy said more doubtfully: "The cows will have gone wild."

"Shouldn't be too difficult to catch a few, and tame them again."

"And then there's milking."

"I managed to milk a cow I found wandering, in the early days," Neil said. "They'll have gone out of milk, of course, but they'll come back in when they calve. We just need to find one that's in calf."

"The whole idea's silly," Billie said.

"I don't see why," Neil said.

"Because it is. Stupid!"

She was suddenly voluble, pouring scorn on the suggestion, haranguing them in a grinding monotone. Neil at first attempted some mild objections, hoping to have Lucy support him. But she did not, and after a time he abandoned argument and sat in silence. When Billie at last came to a halt, it was with the authority of an undisputed victor.

The girls shared a room on the same floor, at the back of the house. Lucy made a bed up for Neil on the floor above. Billie made no comment, but her look was unfriendly.

Neil left his door open and could hear them talking. The words were unintelligible, but he could recognize the voices and realized that Billie was doing most of the talking. Putting the case for kicking him out, he guessed, but was too tired to bother much. It was good, after the months of solitude, just to listen to the murmur of voices. And even better, knowing one of them was Lucy's. He drifted into sleep, thinking about that.

TEN

NEIL AWOKE to a feeling of strangeness and slight apprehension, but as he took in the details of the unfamiliar
room and remembered how he had come to be there, it
was replaced by contentment. He stretched out in bed. He
had slept well: it was quite light outside the window, and
birds were making their ordinary daytime noises rather
than the full-throated dawn chorus. He listened:
sparrows, and a blackbird. Apart from that there was
silence all round.

He sat up. Silence. . . . He thought of Billie's open hostility, and the monotonous arguing voice after he had
come to bed. He remembered Lucy's muteness in the face
of her earlier hectoring. There was nothing to have
stopped them moving away while he was asleep. They
would not have been able to take much with them, but
that scarcely mattered in a world where everything was so
easily replaced. And while they would not have been able
to travel far, in the course of a night, there was no shortage
of hiding places. Nor would it be easy to track them down,
now that they were forewarned.

With these thoughts spinning through his mind, Neil

jumped out of bed and pulled clothes on. The stillness seemed more marked as he ran downstairs. He was sure they had gone; equally sure that, though he could well do without Billie, the thought of losing Lucy was unbearable.

He pushed open the door of the sitting room and found it empty. Their bedroom door was already open, and a glance showed that to be empty, too, the beds unmade and abandoned. Neil's pulse hammered as he ran downstairs. Haste was almost certainly pointless – they would have left hours ago – but he could not help himself. He pulled open the front door and saw, as expected, an empty street. He was staring out, wondering what to do next, when his name was called.

"Neil? What *are* you up to?"

Lucy stood at the top of the stairs. She was wearing brown slacks and a cherry-red jumper: a glow of brightness. Neil went slowly back.

He said: "I thought you'd gone."

"Gone?"

He looked at her. "Run away."

She shook her head, smiling. "I was in the kitchen, cleaning up."

He felt a fool. "I didn't look there."

"I've finished, more or less. Would you like some breakfast?" She paused. "Billie's gone out."

Neil sat on a stool and watched her prepare it. There was an appetizing smell of cooking and coffee. Her movements were quick and deft, and gave him a cosy feeling whose roots seemed to lie a long way back. She was humming as she busied herself, a McCartney tune. He said suddenly:

"It was discussed, wasn't it?"

She half-turned. "What was?"

Her smile was a little lop-sided, he noticed, lifting the left-hand corner of her mouth a fraction more than the right.

"Leaving – while I was asleep."

107

Her look was more serious. "Why do you say that?"

"It's a guess. But not all that clever a one. Billie did her best to get away when I chased her. And then was walking on past here until you called. I suppose she still hoped to ditch me somehow. I could hear her going on at you last night. Wasn't that what she was trying to talk you into?"

She turned back to the primus stove, without answering. Neil said:

"Why is she like that?"

"There's a lot of sense in it. Things *have* changed. You can't be expected to trust strangers."

"But how can you ever come to trust anyone, if you refuse to get to know them?" Lucy did not reply to that, either. "Would you trust me, now?"

She gave a slow nod. "I think so."

"But Billie doesn't?"

"She's more cautious than I am. She's probably right to be."

"It's nothing to do with caution. You know that."

She looked at him across the frying pan.

"What do you mean?"

"It's wanting to keep you to herself—jealousy of anyone else being on the scene."

"That's silly!"

"I don't think so. She sees herself as the protector and organizer. She tells you what to do. And she doesn't want any competition."

Lucy stared at him. Her look, for the first time, had resentment in it.

"Billie's my friend. And I don't need protecting or organizing—not by anybody."

The comment was pointed, and Neil realized he had gone too far. He was silent for some moments, then said:

"At any rate, you didn't let her persuade you to go away. I'm glad."

"I didn't think there was enough reason. We'd have had to find a new place. It would mean a lot of cleaning up and doing. Too much trouble.''

She spoke with indifference, real or assumed. The latter, he hoped, but could not be sure. Their eyes met, and at least the unfriendly look had gone. She said:
"Your breakfast's ready."

During the next few days Neil had to put up with a good deal of harassment from Billie. She was constantly and acidly critical – of things he said, his appearance, habits, practically everything he did.

He realized she was deliberately trying to make him angry and did his best to disregard it, but now and then she succeeded in getting under his skin. One such occasion was when she called him a pig, the word spat out, for failing to wipe his feet properly on the hall mat, and bringing in dirt.

"Look at that!" She pointed to a dab of leafy mud on the carpet. "Really piggish. And when Lucy's spent hours, cleaning it. It's disgusting."

What irritated him was not so much the reproach, nor even the bitterly contemptuous tone, as the fact that Lucy was present; and though she said it didn't matter she had, in fact, shampooed the carpet that morning. Nor had she been able to restrain a momentary look of annoyance, which Billie had also seen with evident satisfaction. The abuse was intended as a reminder of the time when there had been just the two of them, before he blundered on to the scene.

On that occasion as on others Neil managed to bite back the urge to retaliate: he simply apologised to Lucy and held his peace. While he knew where he was with Billie – quite simply she wanted him out – he was not at all sure about Lucy. What was fairly clear was that any sign of aggression towards Billie on his part, however provoked, involved the risk of banding the two girls more closely together.

It was good advice he gave himself, but not easy to

follow. He was thinking about it in bed one night, wondering how long he was going to be able to keep his cool, when he heard the noise outside. It shattered the silence, a loud snarling cough that sent a shiver down his spine. A moment later it came again, louder and nearer. He got up, threw on a dressing gown, and went down to the girls' room.

They were awake and had a light on. They looked scared, but probably he did, too. Lucy said:

"It woke you as well? What was it?"

"I don't know." He hesitated. "It might. . . ."

"What?"

"I was thinking about the Zoo animals. I imagine most of them died of hunger when there was no-one to feed them. But the odd one may have escaped."

The coughing roar came again; it sounded as though it was directly beneath the window.

"What sort of animal?", Lucy asked.

"A big cat, probably. Leopard, maybe." He managed a smile. "I'm not very well up on animal noises."

"It can't get in here," Billie said, "whatever it is."

"No."

For once there was no feeling of hostility. They sat in uneasy silence, listening. Minutes passed and nothing happened. Neil was thinking they might as well go back to bed when there was another sound in the distance, this time a howl of pain. It was repeated a couple of times; then there was quiet again. Lucy looked at him, in query.

"Making its kill," Neil said.

"Of what?"

Billie answered. "A dog," she said flatly.

Neil nodded. "It can't hurt us. Go back to sleep," he said.

In the morning Neil investigated. He did not have to look far. The carcass, or what was left of it, lay at the corner of the street. Most had been eaten; only the hindquarters remained. It had been a dog, all right, but not the

110

small terrier he had imagined. The hindquarters were of something big and hairy – a sheepdog possibly.

Suppressing nausea, Neil dragged the remains into a nearby garden and left them out of sight behind a bush. Scavengers, the rats in particular, would soon dispose of them. He kept a wary eye open on the way back to the house. Anything capable of killing a dog of that size was as likely to attack a human being. Presumably it was not hungry at the moment, but the thought did not completely reassure him.

After washing he gave the girls a brief account. He did not mention how big the dog had been, but he did say:

"I think we ought to have some sort of protection, a weapon, in case it comes back."

Billie automatically began pouring scorn on the idea: there was no reason to think it would come back – they had never heard it before – and it hunted by night, and they were safe in the house, anyway.

Neil ignored her, and spoke to Lucy:

"There was a revolver, and bullets, in the place where I lived. I didn't have any use for them then, so I left them there. But I think it might not be a bad idea to go over and pick them up."

Billie said, with contempt: "It really did scare you!"

He was looking at Lucy. She nodded slightly.

"Yes. I think that's a good idea."

It was the first time she had come out positively on his side. Billie was silenced. He said:

"I'll go over there right away."

Neil found the revolver in the drawer where he had left it. There were three boxes of bullets, two sealed, one opened but nearly full. He filled the barrel and stowed the rest away. More than enough for the present; and if he did need more it should not be difficult to find a gunsmith. The Yellow Pages would help him to locate one.

If he did, it occurred to him, he could also pick up other

111

weapons. A shot-gun would be useful for killing game, if they went out into the country. He had a sudden feeling of optimism about that. If Lucy had sided with him against Billie once, she might do again.

He came out on to the landing with the gun in his hand. Portrait oil paintings lined the hall below and ascended the wall of the broad oak staircase. There was a large window at the top, but the day was grey outside and the faces looked shadowy and unreal. They had been very important people, no doubt, in those days when things like class and rank and wealth had meaning.

One of the nearer ones, he thought, resembled Billie slightly – a woman with a pointed face and staring eyes. He realized he had not yet tried firing the gun. He raised it at arm's length and drew a bead on the glimmering forehead. The crash, and the jerk of the weapon forcing his hand up, startled him. He could not see whether he had hit the picture, and did not stay to look. His ears were deafened, and he felt a bit ashamed of himself as he put the gun in his pocket.

He went through to his own old quarters, where there were things he wanted to collect: his cassette player, which was better than the one the girls had, and various items of food to add to the communal stock, including Swiss chocolates he thought Lucy might like. He filled the rucksack with what he needed.

It was strange being back. He remembered *The Wind in the Willows*, and Mole's wretchedness when he took Ratty back to his abandoned house. This place had never really been a home to him, but seeing it again produced a sense of dreariness and depression.

There seemed to be dust everywhere. There probably always had been: he was viewing it through eyes that had become re-accustomed to feminine standards of cleanliness. The large spider's web occupying one corner, on the other hand, was definitely new. But it was not those things, nor the cold grey ashes in the hearth, which made him marvel at the thought that he had once lived here, and believed himself reasonably content. It was the silence, the crushing awareness of solitude, which did that. He felt a compulsion to break the stillness – to say something, anything. He found himself calling Lucy's name.

His voice sounded like that of a stranger; and the silence which settled back seemed even heavier, more pervading. In it, the thought that suddenly came to him seemed to ring like a cracked discordant bell. How long had he been away from the girls – two hours, three? The first time, anyway, for more than a few minutes since he had joined them. Would they be there when he returned?

Night after night he had heard them talking, their voices low and indistinguishable. He had not discussed it with Lucy again, but there was every chance that Billie had been plugging the same theme – arguing the case for their giving him the slip and going away together. And was it unreasonable that in the end she should have prevailed? He had no clear idea of what Lucy felt about him; but when he criticized Billie to her, she had been quick to resent it, telling him Billie was her friend. A dominant friend: it was Billie who had organized concealment, Billie who had decided they should make no response to the bell-ringing.

The very thing about which he had been so pleased – Lucy's agreeing with him about getting the revolver – could have been a calculated deceit: the means by which they could secure his absence from the house long enough to give them a good start; and in daylight. They could be miles away by now, lost beyond hope of rediscovery.

Abandoning the rucksack, Neil raced out of the house. The car stood outside, where he had left it over a week before. He flung himself into the driver's seat and turned the key. The starter whirred, but nothing happened; and the same at the second attempt. He remembered that petrol had been low – that he had been meaning to get more but had left it while he made his search on foot through Chelsea.

A bicycle he had occasionally used was propped in the hall. One of the tyres was flat; he found his fingers all thumbs as he fitted the pump to the valve. It seemed ages before the tyre was inflated, and he could get on the bicycle and pedal away.

The sense of loss, the misery, was much worse than on that first morning after meeting her. He had a chest-pinching sense of desperation, a sickness in the stomach, an overwhelming need to gulp air. It was partly physical, then entirely so. As he passed the vacant hulk of a Green Line bus, halted forever outside the Brompton Oratory, cramp struck, a crippling pain that bit into his side. He had to dismount and wait, doubled over, for it to go away.

The enforced delay gave him a chance to think more clearly, despite the pain. He saw Lucy again in his mind's eye and realized how absurd his imagining had been. It did not matter about Billie; he knew Lucy would not have betrayed him like that. The agony of cramp had ebbed. He straightened up and took a tentative breath, followed by a deeper one. Then he remounted the bicycle and rode on, no longer in a hurry.

He met Billie first, at the top of the stairs. She said, with a note of disgust:

"You're back sooner than we thought."

He said indifferently: "Am I? Where's Lucy?"

She came out of the kitchen: all blue, in a guernsey with slacks of a lighter shade. She looked at him, past Billie.

"You're back!"

The words were the same, the intonation very different. Neil grinned cheerfully at her.

"Yes. I'm back."

Billie next morning went foraging on her own, and returned excited over a discovery. She burst into the sitting room where Neil and Lucy were having coffee, and talked about it volubly. She had been exploring westwards

114

along the river bank and had found, in a small house in the poor area around Lots Road, an old-fashioned treadle sewing machine. As far as she could tell, it was in perfect working order. There was a pile of mending on the table beside it which showed that it had been in use.

Neil gathered, as she went on, that this was meant to represent the fulfilment of a long-standing desire of Lucy's. Apparently dress-making had been a hobby of hers in the past; and on some occasion she had expressed frustration to Billie over the fact that, while sewing machines were available for the taking, they were all useless without electrical power.

It would be easy enough, Billie suggested, to bring it over in a wheelbarrow: the house was not much more than a quarter of a mile away. She looked at Lucy expectantly; like a dog, Neil thought, expecting to be patted for performing a trick.

Lucy said: "Well, thank you, Billie, but. . . ."

"I could get it this afternoon."

"I'm not sure it would be worth it, until things are more settled."

"More settled? How?"

"If we're going to move out into the country eventually. . . . I think Neil's probably right about that. We ought to start taking a longer view of things – plan for the future. And we'll need to travel as lightly as possible when we do move. For that matter, it probably won't be difficult to find an old sewing machine outside London. There were two in my village that I know of."

Neil waited for Billie's reaction, expecting a heated argument at the least. But she merely stared at Lucy in silence for some moments; then said, in a quieter voice than usual:

"I think I'll make some tea."

She walked heavily away towards the kitchen. Neil watched her go very cheerfully.

ELEVEN

BILLIE was not abashed for long. That evening after supper she came into the sitting room from the kitchen to find Neil playing a Stones tape on the recorder, and launched a bitter attack. He had no consideration, she said: he was always playing some horrible row or other. She was sick and tired of the Rolling Stones, and the rest of them. And he might at least turn the volume down.

As far as Neil could see, Billie didn't really like music at all. She had a few tapes which she occasionally put on, of fife and drum music and Scottish ballads, and she would sit tapping her foot throughout, just out of time. He put his hand to the volume switch, and then changed his mind. Lucy quite liked the Stones; he saw no reason why they both should be deprived because Billie was tone-deaf.

He said as much, and the argument started. It raged till Lucy came in, when they both appealed to her. She said:

"We could have it a bit lower, Neil, couldn't we?"

He was willing to oblige her, and the volume *was* too high unless you were listening by yourself. He turned it down, and was rewarded by a smile from Lucy. Billie, though, was not satisfied. She turned from music to the fact that he had not helped with the washing up. Neil said hotly:

"I offered. Lucy told me to go and sit down."

"And you were quick enough to do it!"

"I'd rather he did. There isn't room for three of us out there," Lucy said.

"I don't see why he shouldn't take his turn."

"Does it matter about turns? Look, I'll do it by myself in future. I'd rather."

That didn't suit Billie, either. "No, you won't. I just don't see why he should get away with things."

Lucy managed to calm things down, but another row flared up later when Neil said something which Billie took to be a criticism of North Country people. That one raged until bedtime, and started afresh the following morning.

The difference, Neil recognized, lay on his side. Previously he had put up with Billie's criticisms and insults, out of fear that Lucy might side with her and yield to her pressure to abandon him. He was confident now that that wouldn't happen, and saw no reason why Billie should rant at him unchallenged.

Lucy made it plain that she detested these scenes, and did her best to stop them. Neil himself did make some effort not to get involved, but without much success. The trouble was that Billie had a knack of needling him which he found unendurable. He found everything about her – appearance, voice, the way she stamped across the room so that the floor boards creaked – intensely irritating. The detestation, he was fairly sure, was mutual.

Hostilities dragged on for days, and culminated in the most blazing row of all, which started quite innocently. Billie during supper spoke of going next day to the bookshop in the King's Road: she was running short of reading matter. Neil, bearing in mind an appeal Lucy had made to him earlier to keep the peace, was doing his best to preserve harmony. He suggested they might all go along: there were some books he wanted, too.

The ridiculous starting point was that he, naturally, said 'books' in the southern way, with the short vowel as opposed to the long diphthong Billie had used. She chose to think that he was correcting her accent, trying to be superior, and said so. The fact that he had been bending over backwards not to cause trouble made Neil angrier than usual. In no time the battle was underway, with Lucy's appeals and remonstrances falling on two sets of deaf ears. This time no holds at all were barred, and they gave full vent to their loathing for one another. The verbal battle raged on until Lucy suddenly got up and said, in a strained trembling voice quite unlike her normal tone:

"I can't stand this. I'm going to bed."

She left the room and Billie and Neil sat for some minutes in silence. Then, without speaking, he left her and went to his own room.

It was some time before Neil got to sleep, and when he did he slept heavily. He was awakened by someone tugging at his arm, and realized simultaneously that it was broad daylight and that Billie was bending over him. He wondered hazily if she had come upstairs to continue the row, and struggled to sit up. Her face was tense, but with something other than anger. She was talking but he couldn't properly make her out. He said:

"What's that?"

"Wake *up*. I said it's Lucy. She's not here. She's gone."

She told him more while he pulled clothes on. She had wakened earlier, at first light, and seen Lucy moving about. She had asked what she was doing, and Lucy had told her to go back to sleep: it was just that she was feeling restless. This was not particularly unusual – Lucy was a light sleeper and sometimes did get up very early – and Billie had turned over and slept on. But when she had finally woken properly and got up herself there was no sign of Lucy in the house.

"She's probably gone for a breath of fresh air," Neil

said. He looked out of the window into wintry sunlight. "It's quite a fine day."

"That's what I thought," Billie said. "I waited for her to come back. But it was over an hour ago, and she hasn't."

She looked more nervous than he had seen her; frightened almost. He realized she would have had to be alarmed to have wakened him. He said, feeling the beginning of apprehension himself:

"We'll go out and call for her."

The street showed its usual shabby emptiness. They stood in front of the house, and called in turn. Nothing answered but a screaming gull.

The sun shone still and the morning was not too cold, but clouds were building up over the roofs westwards. Neil thought of Lucy the previous afternoon, pleading with him not to get into another fight with Billie, and of the tremor in her voice when she said: "I can't stand this. . . ." He turned to Billie:

"We'd better go and look for her."

"Where?"

"Well, round here, to start with."

A quarter of an hour of searching and calling brought no result. Then Neil had an idea:

"The bookshop. . . ."

Billie nodded. "She might have gone up there. We'd better take the bikes."

That was when they found the bicycle Lucy used was missing. They took their own and rode to the King's Road bookshop together. There was no sign of her; no answer when, in turn, they called her name. They looked at one another. Billie's face was strained. She was going to blame him, Neil thought – say how everything had been all right until he came. He did not care if she did: nothing mattered except the fact that Lucy was missing. But instead she said:

"Swears & Wells. . . ."

"What?"

"We were talking the other day about fur coats, with the winter setting in. She said we ought to go to Oxford Street, and choose some."

Neil nodded. Anything was better than standing here.

"Right. Let's go."

They cycled, in silence but side by side, through Knightsbridge and across the park to Marble Arch; then down the gloomy canyon of Oxford Street. Swears & Wells, when they reached it, was as blank and forbidding as all the other department stores. Moreover its doors were locked, and there was no sign of a forced entry. They checked all round, then stood together on the pavement under a lowering sky. Neil said:

"We might as well get back."

Billie said nothing, but nodded. She looked as though she might be going to cry. He got on his bicycle, and she followed him.

They had not gone much more than a hundred yards before it started raining – a few heavy spots, soon turning into a drenching downpour. They had to take shelter in the doorway of one of the shops. It was a photographer's, the window full of expensive-looking cameras. In front of them the rain sheeted down and the gutter soon was running full. Lightning flashed, and he saw Billie shiver when the thunder followed.

He supposed he ought to console her, with words if nothing else, but the thought was unbearable. Earlier he had been able to forget his dislike; there had even been some sense of alliance since they were both seeking the same person. Now, inactive because of the rain, he was forced to think about Lucy, and the more he thought the more frightened he became.

It had been absurd to imagine she had gone on a foraging expedition of her own, either to the bookshop or the furriers. It was not the sort of thing she would do. Nor, he was sure now, had she abandoned them because of the bad feeling between Billie and him. And if neither of those explanations for her being missing was right, there seemed only one possibility: that something had happened to her.

She had gone out early, and taken her bicycle. In the morning dusk she might not have seen a pothole in the road, might have fallen and twisted an ankle – maybe broken a leg. He thought of that, willing it to be so, to keep the other image out of his mind. But it would not be rejected: he saw her cycling, saw the spotted beast lurking in the shadows, crouching, springing. . . .

Billie said: "Oh God, I wish it'd stop."

Neil did not answer. He hated her more than ever – for having gone back to sleep when Lucy went out, for having suggested this wild goose chase into central London . . . for being alive when Lucy might be dead. It was irrational, he realized, but he could not help it.

The rain slackened at last, and by unspoken agreement they got back on their bicycles and headed west. A thin drizzle persisted, and Neil was soon soaked to the skin. He did not mind the discomfort, welcomed it even: to some extent it stopped him thinking.

They abandoned their bicycles outside the house. Following Billie up the steps to the front door, Neil thought of what he was going to do. A quick rub-down, dry clothes and waterproofs, and out again. If anything had happened to her. . . .

He heard Billie's exclamation of relief as he reached the top of the stairs. It was only then he noticed there were lights on in the sitting room, and felt the warmth from the paraffin heater. He ran the last few steps, jostling Billie as he entered. Lucy was in her usual armchair, sewing.

Billie said: "What happened to you? We thought. . . ."

She did not finish the sentence. Lucy said:

"It was a fine morning, so I went for a ride. I got as far as Chiswick Reach. I was luckier than you – I got back just before the rain started. You're both drenched. Go and

121

change, and I'll put the kettle on."

Neil was not alone with Lucy until the following morning when Billie made her delayed expedition to the bookshop. Neil did not, on this occasion, volunteer to go with her. She asked Lucy if she wanted to come. With satisfaction, Neil heard Lucy say:

"I don't think so, today. I've got things I want to do." She smiled at Billie. "If you see a new cookbook that might be useful you can bring me it."

When Billie had clattered down the stairs and the front door had closed behind her, Neil said:

"Why did you do it?"

"Do what?"

"Go out on your own yesterday morning."

"I told you – it was a fine morning, I felt like a ride."

She had a strange look: defensive, distant. It made him feel defensive himself, and slightly nettled. He said:

"You could have left a message. We were worried about you."

"I didn't mean to be gone long."

"But you were."

She paused. "I wanted to think about things."

"What things?"

"Just things."

Her evasiveness irritated him further. He said, aware of the sharpness in his voice:

"You should have thought of us – wondering what had happened to you."

She looked at him in silence for a moment. In a small cold voice, she said:

"Perhaps I should. I'm sorry." She didn't sound sorry. Her voice still colder, she said: "Weren't you going to see to that broken window?"

She turned away and went into the kitchen, where he heard the sound of pans being vigorously cleaned. He resented that, too, and the cutting little reminder about the window. He angrily set about getting the materials together and went to work on the glass. It was a poor way of spending one of the rare hours without Billie on the scene, but that was Lucy's fault.

His anger evaporated while he worked. It didn't matter whose fault it was; the point was that minutes were passing and all too soon Billie would be back. He finished puttying the glass, wiped his hands on a rag, and walked towards the kitchen.

He was halfway across the sitting room when Lucy entered it. They stopped and looked at each other. She still had that strange look. She said scoldingly:

"You've got putty on your shirt."

She came and stood in front of him and put her hand to his sleeve. The smell of the scent she wore mingled with the oily smell of putty. He put his hand on her shoulders, felt her draw back, but caught and kissed her all the same.

She was very still. He had the feeling he had ruined everything. She pulled back again, and he let her go. He said, as awkward as the kiss had been:

"I'm sorry."

She was smiling, and shaking her head.

He looked over her shoulder when they separated again. Billie was standing at the top of the stairs; for once she had come up quietly.

TWELVE

BILLIE MADE NO COMMENT, then or later. Lucy, when she was briefly absent, said to him:

"Try to make things easy for her."

"Billie?"

"Yes."

"If she'll let me."

"She knows she's . . . a spare part. We mustn't rub it in."

Neil liked hearing her say "we." And in his present mood anything Lucy wanted he wanted. He said:

"I'll do what I can. It'll be difficult. She'll hate me more than ever now."

But to his surprise Billie's attitude had changed. The sniping and criticism stopped completely. She appeared to go out of her way to be amiable to him. When the project for moving to the country was brought up again, she supported it enthusiastically. Almost too enthusiastically: she put forward ideas and suggestions without hostility but with a noisy assurance that Neil thought was even more irritating.

He much preferred to talk about it in the rare moments

of being alone with Lucy. Spring was the obvious time for the move, and they considered the various possibilities. The difficulty was in deciding which to choose. In the end they agreed they would head first towards Oxfordshire. That was Neil's idea: he wanted to see the countryside in which Lucy had grown up.

Later, they thought, they would wander westwards, into the Cotswolds. They had a feeling, persuasive because they shared it, that they would find what they were looking for among the honey-coloured villages and farmhouses deep in those friendly hills. Billie reappeared at that point, and Neil did what he could to look pleasant. It wasn't easy.

Nor did it get easier. He was able to control himself when Lucy was present, but increasingly when he was alone with Billie he found himself snapping at her. The fact that she accepted this meekly did not improve matters. He grew to loathe her subservience even more than he had her brashness and hostility. He tried to take refuge in blankness, in not responding to her in any way, but it didn't work. The fact was that every moment of her being there was a moment in which he could not be alone with Lucy. And this was something which would continue indefinitely. In the old world there would have been some hope of escape: there was none here. The sight of her coming into the room, her footsteps on the stairs, set his teeth on edge.

Billie had kept a record of the passing days; she had hung up a calendar on the sitting room wall and punctiliously marked it each morning. So it was she who drew their attention to the approach of Christmas. She was insistent on making it an occasion, and proposed an expedition so that they could get presents to give one another.

Neil thought it pointless, and said so to Lucy. She nodded.

"I know. We've got all we need. But let's humour her. Please?"

He shrugged. "All right. But don't expect a tiara."

She caught his hand, smiling. "I won't."

They went to Bond Street together; then separated to make their choices. Neil was soon back at the rendezvous, and waited restlessly until Lucy joined him. He was uneasy about her being away even for half an hour; he had wanted her to take the gun but she had firmly refused.

Billie was the last to return, and looked pleased with herself. She cycled ahead of them as they made their way back against a biting wind, singing, or rather shouting carols as she went. That evening – Christmas Eve, she reminded them – she played carols on the cassette player, well beyond the point of boredom.

They exchanged presents the following morning. Lucy had got a silver-backed brush and mirror set for Billie, and Neil gave her soft leather boots. Her presents to them, not just gift-wrapped but decorated with a profusion of seals and ribbons, were far more magnificent: for Neil a gold Swiss chronometer, showing the time all over the world, attached to a gold bracelet which it was a distinct effort to lift; for Lucy, a necklace of diamonds and sapphires.

Finally they opened their presents to each other. Neil had got a small book of love poems for Lucy while hers to him was as simple: a set of detailed maps of England.

"So you can find the way for us," she said, smiling. "I thought of getting a compass, as well, but I didn't see one."

Billie's exuberance faded, and was replaced by a moroseness that lasted the rest of the day. Neil wondered if she thought they had actually planned to mock her costly gifts by the modesty of their own to one another. He couldn't help being pleased about it. It was another sign of the closeness between him and Lucy, a further reminder that where two was company, three was none.

Lucy did her best to sustain a festive spirit by cooking

126

them a special meal, finishing with plum pudding and brandy sauce; and producing a box of crackers to go with it. They all put on paper hats but it was hopeless. Billie sat most of the time without speaking, and went early to bed.

Snow came soon after; at first in a flurry that melted as it fell but later in a steady down-drift settling more and more thickly on roofs and ledges and pavements. It snowed all day and much of the night; then, after a dry grey morning with the wind whipping fallen snow into drifts against the walls, it set in again.

The blizzard continued off and on for several days, and afterwards the going was too difficult to venture far. They only went out to collect snow to melt: the pipes had frozen and taps were no longer working. Most of the time they were obliged to stay indoors.

During this period of confinement, Neil found Billie getting on his nerves worse than ever. She had got over her sulks and was trying to be helpful but there was something about her appearance of cheerfulness that maddened him. She had always had an annoying habit of whistling through her teeth: now she did it almost continuously, and always the same tune – "The Cock o' the North," off-key. In the end, when Lucy was in the kitchen, he said to her in a low but savage voice:

"If you don't stop that whistling, I swear I'll kill you! I mean it."

She looked at him, crestfallen. "I'm sorry, Neil."

He turned away without answering. Even his own name, spoken in her voice, rasped on his nerves.

Next morning, though, they awoke to bright sunshine, and the sound of water dripping from the eaves. The thaw was rapid, and by mid-day the roads were passable. Billie, euphoric again, proposed that she and Neil make an expedition to the Supermarket.

"Do we need to?" He looked at Lucy. "How are supplies?"

"Low in cooking oil and nearly out of potatoes. But we could manage for a couple of days."

"It might snow again," Billie said.

"Doesn't look like it."

Neil pointed to the unblemished blue above the roofs opposite. Billie said:

"I don't think we ought to take a chance on that."

Lucy nodded at him from behind her, urging him to be accommodating. He said:

"All right. I'll come with you."

He slipped the gun into his anorak pocket before leaving the house; it had become a routine action by now. Outside it was even better than it looked: a mild spring-like day with water gurgling in the gutters. There were patches of snow in places, but not enough to impede their bicycles.

They rode side by side and Billie chattered cheerfully at first. Neil did not respond – he did not feel like it and Lucy wasn't there to spur him – and after a time Billie fell silent, too.

They parked their bicycles and Neil pushed open the door of the Supermarket. A window had collapsed during the blizzard and snow had drifted in. It was melting messily, with soggy cornflake packets sticking out like artificial boulders. Year by year, of course, the ruin would increase and spread – the winters dragging things down, and spring and summer turning seeds into saplings and finally into foundation-wrenching trees. But it wouldn't matter: they would be a long way from here, in a place where nature could be tamed.

He and Billie had split up. He heard her moving about in the kitchenware department, and remembered her talking of getting Lucy a new casserole dish to replace one that had cracked. He put a tin of oil and half a dozen tins of potatoes by the door, where they could be easily picked up, and wandered along the aisles to see if there was anything else worth taking. Sardines: they must be getting low on them. He scooped up tins, and carried them over to

128

put with the rest.

He heard Billie coming while he was bending over the stack of tins. He paid little attention, but then was struck by something: her footsteps had a quieter, more purposeful tread than usual. He straightened up, and turned to look. As he did, she rushed the last few paces, the kitchen knife bright in her upraised hand.

Neil tried to fling himself to one side, but she was too close. He felt the blow on his chest, seeming to punch more than stab, and staggered, almost falling. But he could still think clearly. He thrust a hand in his pocket, and found the butt of the revolver.

Billie came at him again. Her face was strained, as though she were concentrating hard. He pressed the trigger, heard the hammer click futilely, and was just in time to throw up his left hand and grasp the wrist of the hand that held the knife.

He managed to divert that blow, but she was struggling to get at him and her strength surprised and shocked him. They swayed together, and he felt the warmth of her breath. His chest felt as though a heavy weight was pressing against it. He had a frightening sense of weakness, a despairing conviction that she had him at her mercy, and would show none.

Unexpectedly he had a recollection of the last time he had wrestled with someone – his brother Andy, on a Sunday morning, with his father calling out to them to keep quiet. On that occasion he had been in the ascendancy, until Andy suddenly switched from push to pull and, caught off balance, he had crashed across the bed on to the floor. He tried it now, yielding to Billie's straining effort, dodging, and wrenching hard. She came flying past him and slammed into a display shelf. Bottles of sauce and tubes of tomato puree cascaded round her as she fell.

Neil did not wait for her to get up. He ran for the door, grabbed his bicycle, and pedalled away. The weight on his chest was turning into pain, and he had noticed red specks in the drift of snow outside the Supermarket door. At the corner he risked a look back, but there was no-one in sight. The pain was worse and so was the feeling of weakness, but he forced his legs to pedal faster.

He was even more faint by the time he reached the house and pushed home the bolt inside the door. He leaned against it for a moment, clutching his chest. There was blood around the gaping slit in the anorak and on his trousers. Drops spotted the carpet as he went upstairs.

Lucy's face whitened when she saw him.

"You're hurt! What happened?"

He told her, briefly; it was painful to talk, even to breathe. She led him to the bathroom, supporting him, and eased off the anorak and the bloody shirt underneath. Although very pale, she was calm. She examined the wound closely.

"It's nasty," she said. "But not deep. It must have slid off your ribs."

"She meant to stab me in the back." He winced. "She would have, if I hadn't turned to face her."

"I'll sponge it. With antiseptic. It's going to hurt, I'm afraid."

She busied herself at the medicine chest while Neil held a towel to stanch the blood. He said:

"I wonder how long she's been planning that?"

"It was probably on impulse – a sort of brain-storm."

Neil reached painfully into his pocket, and produced the gun. He flicked the barrel.

"Empty. She'd taken the bullets out."

Lucy stared at him. "Then she really meant to kill you. . . ."

Her face had tightened; it was as though she only now grasped what had happened. Neil nodded.

"I bolted the door downstairs."

"And almost succeeded!" Lucy drew in breath, a small wail of horror. "You'd have been dead."

130

He managed a smile. "I'm not, though. Ready with the sulphuric acid?"

It was more painful than he had expected, and he could not help crying out at one point. Lucy looked at him with concern, but carried on with the cleansing until she was satisfied she had done a thorough job. The rest, the dressing and bandaging, was comparatively easy going. Afterwards she sat him in an armchair while she made tea.

Neil said: "I was ready for that." He sipped it. "Whew! Brandy?"

She nodded. "I thought you needed something."

"Good," he said appreciatively. He felt it warming him. "I wonder where she is. Or how she is. It was a heavy fall and might have knocked her out. I didn't stay to check."

"I hope she's dead."

It was said calmly, but with conviction. Neil moved in the chair, and felt the pain pull at him.

"I don't think she'll come back here. But just in case she does. . . ."

"We mustn't take chances."

It was odd, hearing the echo of Billie's remark about food supplies; odder to realize that had been only about an hour ago. He said:

"Bullets. On the bookcase shelf. Can you bring me a box?"

He reloaded the gun, and felt safer. Lucy said:

"She might try again. She could be lying in wait for you – anywhere, any time. We'll move, as soon as you're fit to travel."

"I'm fit now."

"No." Her tone admitted no argument. "In a day or two, maybe."

As the afternoon faded they sat and talked; about the future chiefly, about the place they were going to find, and what they would make of it. A vegetable garden, a potato patch, an orchard with apple- and pear-trees, cherries

131

and plums and damsons. Eventually, maybe, a wheatfield, and they would grind corn and make their own bread. And animals, of course: hens, pigs, a small herd of cattle. Hard work, but worth the effort.

And it was a future, too, from which an unpleasant cloud had lifted. There was a positive joy for Neil in the thought of not hearing the flat voice grinding on, the heavy unmistakeable thump of her footsteps.

But, more important still, having Lucy to himself. She had come to sit on the rug beside his chair, her head against his knee. He stroked the soft hair, and felt her press back on to his hand.

It was all going to be marvellous, he thought contentedly, and was checked by a stab of pain. But that had been worth it. This would not be happening if Billie hadn't tried to kill him. Much more than worth it.

Lucy said: "We ought to get to a good bookshop before we leave London. Foyle's, maybe."

"Ought we? There are bookshops outside London. And we don't want to have too much to lug around."

"Not so comprehensive. We want books on farming. Even though my father worked on a farm, I know next to nothing about it. He wasn't much of a talker, of course. There'll be a lot to learn."

"Yes." He gently tugged her hair. "Clever Lucy."

"I'd like us to have a pond. So we can have ducks."

"Yes." A thought struck him. "Have you done any horse-riding?"

"A bit. Have you?"

"No. You'll have to teach me."

She laughed. "A bit, I said! Not enough to teach anybody."

"We'll learn together, then. It's going to be our best way of getting around."

"They'll have gone wild."

"We'll catch them and tame them again. Like the cows."

Everything seemed simple; and if it weren't, it didn't matter. They sat in easy silence. The windows were getting quite dark. Lucy said: "I'd better be seeing to supper," but did not stir. Then, in a changed voice, she said:

"What's that?"

Neil listened. It came from somewhere outside, a low keening sound. Too loud for a cat, and different. The wild beast? It became louder still. He got out of the chair and went to the window. Pain struck him as he tried to lift the sash, and Lucy said:

"Let me do it."

The weather was clear but cold; there would be frost soon if it weren't freezing already. Together they looked out of the window. The moaning was coming from a dark shape, sitting huddled against the gatepost.

She had heard the sound of the window being opened. She looked up at them.

"Let me in. Please! Oh, please. . . ."

Lucy slammed the window shut. They stood close, and he could feel her shivering. The voice went on; fainter, but still intelligible.

"I'm sorry. I won't again. I promise. Don't leave me out here. Please, let me in! For God's sake. . . ."

Neil looked at Lucy in the dusk of the room.

"She tried to kill you." Her voice was hard and certain.

Neil thought about Billie. She was not to be trusted. Whatever she said now, there was the chance of it happening again. He would need to watch out for her every minute of the day. And even then he could never be sure of being safe.

The crying, begging, protestations went on. Letting her in meant letting her into the dream as well – subjecting it to the grind of that voice, the stamp of those feet. And putting everything – the future, life itself – at risk.

Take no chances: that was the sensible principle for life in an empty world. And he need do nothing but sit tight.

She would have to go eventually, to find shelter for the night. They could carry out their plan, and slip away. She would never find them.

Lucy said, as though echoing his thought:

"She'll go away soon."

It would be easy. The dream would become a reality – for the two of them, with no unwelcome third. He moved from the window, and Lucy went with him. The cries continued, but more distantly. One could ignore them for now, and tomorrow they would be miles away.

Billie would manage. Things were no worse for her than they had been for him on his own. Take no chances: too much was at stake. He looked at Lucy and knew she was his, wholly. You're a winner, he told himself. Losers are losers – and she did try to kill you.

The voice was raised again, but she could not keep it up indefinitely. If they went into the kitchen or the back room, and closed the door. . . .

It was no use. If they travelled to the opposite end of England those cries would ring in his mind, and go on ringing through the years ahead. It did not matter what the chances were, nor how much was at stake. All that counted was the emptiness of the world, and that she was human and alone.

He looked at Lucy. "It's no good."

She asked no question; just nodded. One of the many good things that were there, and would continue. Neil pressed her arm, and went downstairs to let Billie in.